# A Groom for Altar

## The Blizzard Brides Series, #7

# Parker J. Cole

# Copyright Information
Copyright © 2021 Parker J. Cole
Cover Art by EDH Graphics

# CONTENTS

# Dedication

*To the Author and Finisher of my faith who has shown me throughout the most difficult and the most rewarding year of my life to date, that He knows who I am, and that more than anyone in the world, He loves me.*

*And she [Delilah] said unto him [Samson], How canst thou say, I love thee, when thine heart is not with me? Thou hast mocked me these three times, and hast not told me wherein thy great strength lieth.*

*And it came to pass, when she pressed him daily with her words, and urged him, so that his soul was vexed unto death;*

*That he told her all his heart, and said unto her, There hath not come a razor upon mine head; for I have been a Nazarite unto God from my mother's womb: if I be shaven, then my strength will go from me, and I shall become weak, and be like any other man.*

Judges 16: 15-17

# <u>Prologue</u>

*Last Chance, Nebraska*
*September 1878*

Rays of waning sunlight dappled the surface of North Platte River. Water crested and gulped at the edges of the pier. The man stared at the ripples, his eyes fixed not on the water, but on the bodies only he could see underneath it.

Bloated figures and bulging eyes gazing blankly up at him.

Sucking in a breath, he squatted down, and his hand reached down to touch them, to make sure that no matter what, they were still there under the river. Hidden in their soggy graves from the people who once loved them.

Once? No, not once. The people who *still* loved them.

The man's hands broke through the thin, fluid surface. Although he could see the inert corpses, for some reason, he was unable to touch them.

He *had* to touch them, had to make sure they were fish food, monster bait, or whatever else the claims of a watery death would make them. They had to stay there, where no one could ever find them.

Only then would he find peace.

He bent down further, the water reaching to the bend of his elbow. How could this be? The bodies still lay close to the surface, not unlike a twisted version of a child's eager visage pressed against a shop's window. Yet, he hadn't touched them.

The water now came to his armpits and no contact. What was going on? Now on his stomach, both arms fully submerged into the water, he swished the water back and forth, desperate to grab hold of them.

He stared at their dull faces, seeing their features etched clearly except for the unnatural swelling of their cheeks. They had once been beautiful people.

It was his fault they no longer were.

The bodies broke the veil of their grave, bobbing to the surface like a pair of buoys. Fear ate at his insides and with a harsh dry sob, he frantically tried to push them back under the water.

But he couldn't reach them. Couldn't touch them.

His lips pulled back from his teeth as the bodies seemed to float up into the air, so close their noses almost touched.

Now his sunken arms were incapable of movement. Imprisoned, just like the bodies he had put there. Why couldn't he get out of the water?

Air seesawed out of his mouth. He wiggled like a fish trying to escape the hook.

The faces of the dead, so close, stared unseeing.

Then, four pairs of lifeless eyes blinked.

The man jerked awake, gasping, and gulping in air. His heart slammed inside his chest, threatening to beat a hasty exit. Light perspiration beaded his brow and upper lip along with a gluey string of snot. Wiping it all away with the sleeve of his shirt, he collapsed back on the chair and sighed.

He glanced out of the tiny window. Late afternoon. It would be time to go back home soon.

His eyes drifted back down to the letter he'd written before he'd fallen asleep. He silently mouthed the first line.

*My sin is ever before me.*

He glanced around to see the bunkhouse was blessedly empty. Had it been that way while he slept, or had someone come in, read his letter and then—

No, that's not what happened. He'd fallen asleep on top of it, arms crossed, and his head cushioned on top of them. No one had seen it.

Why wasn't he relieved then?

The man took the letter and the envelope and folded one into another. Then he folded the envelope and placed it in the waist band of his pants, under his shirt where the edges of it poked his back.

Like a knife.

He gathered his belongings and stood up just as the door opened.

"You still here?"

"Not anymore," he joked, the effortless smile he'd perfected shielding the turmoil inside. "I'm heading for home now."

"All right then. Tell your missus I said hello."

The man nodded, knowing that was the last thing he would do. "Sure will."

# **<u>Chapter One</u>**

*November 1878*
*Thanksgiving Day*

A torrent of invisible fists bludgeoned Altar Pennington's lower back. Hot tears trailed a path down her cheeks as she fell to her knees on the hardwood floor. Her groans echoed in the spartan house as the horror of what her pains were came to the forefront.

She was about to give birth to the baby. All alone.

The damp, soiled blue skirt of her dress slapped against her calves as she crawled like a helpless child. More water trailed along her legs and she squeezed her eyes shut.

Wasn't that the sign that the baby was coming?

She had to get some assistance. If she reached the front door, she could open it and cry out for help. Perhaps the neighbors would hear and send for the midwife.

Another blunt rod of pain slammed into her. Altar let out a scream, her hand clumsily reaching behind her to massage the origin of her torture. It felt hard as stone.

All night long as she lay in bed, as the agony increased, she simply thought she was experiencing a terrible backache. For the last few months, her body had been in all sorts of discomfort. What was one more ache?

How could she have known that it was the precursor to childbirth? No one had told her.

Why hadn't she listened to Heather Barnes and accepted the midwife's offer? Through the waves of throbbing misery sweeping her body, she heard Heather's voice in her head.

"Altar, are you sure? The babe could arrive any day. I can stay with you for a few days until—"

"No, it's quite all right. I'll be fine. You should be enjoying the holiday with your—"

Abruptly, Altar cut off her words. Heather's blue eyes filled with a swift hurt. Of course, Heather wouldn't be enjoying the Thanksgiving holiday.

An awkward hush had fallen upon them as Heather packed her case. "My apologies," she'd offered to the midwife.

Heather pasted a wan smile on her face. "You'd think after several weeks, we'd have had time to get used to the idea. No matter. What does matter is that you are here alone. I wouldn't mind spending a week or so here as I complete my rounds."

"No, please don't. I'm sure the babe will wait until after Thanksgiving to arrive. I'll be fine."

She couldn't have been more wrong.

The hammering at her back eased up. Even that relief caused much anguish, leaving a dreadful ache. Panting, Altar fell to her side and curled into a ball, her hand rested on her swollen belly.

"Oh, dear Lord, it hurts," she moaned out loud.

At least she could take some comfort in the fact that the potential husband she'd written to wouldn't arrive until sometime after the baby's birth. Lying on the floor, she closed her eyes and took in deep breaths.

Two freak blizzards killed many of the women's husbands, including Elbert. Pastor Collins insisted that their widows had to remarry. And soon. Else, they had to leave town.

The overwhelming response after the women advertised their availability resulted in each woman receiving six letters at random. Altar had written to three of the men in quick succession. Two, upon discovering she was Negro, declined to further their acquaintance. The third man's wife had replied, stating her husband wasn't available to be her husband as well.

The fourth letter had a positive response. A man named Wolfe Laingsburg agreed to come and meet her. From there they would decide if marriage would follow.

Frankly, Altar didn't care who she married. Her marriage to Elbert hadn't been spectacular. She doubted marriage to any other man would make a difference.

Her fear lay in raising a child on her own. With no help.

Just as the throbbing eased, it built up again in her back, and she ground her teeth, clenching her fists. Thoughts of her future husband flew away.

Heather had offered to leave some herbs for her to help mitigate her pains, but she had refused them, thinking she'd have time before the baby arrived. How she wished now she'd taken the midwife's offer.

Dizzily, she gazed around her.

Was this the place she was going to raise her baby? This shell of a house, barren of life and love?

She hadn't wanted a child, but God and Elbert had seen to that.

Altar tried to crawl once more, seeing the door not too far from her. The light coming from the crack beneath it blinded her. She squinted, scraping her hands along the floorboards as she pulled herself an inch forward.

Pain, sudden and fierce, sliced through her body. She dropped flat onto the floor.

"Ah! Dear Jesus, please help me. Don't leave me all alone."

Heather tried to tell Altar what to expect, but what could the midwife, who had never had children of her own, understand about the agony of childbirth?

*Must get to the door. Must get help.*

She tried to move again but the pain immobilized her. She whimpered, the sound echoing in the house like a bleat of a sheep.

"I don't want to do this alone. Dear Jesus, please don't let me do this alone."

Just then, an inexplicable urge came over her. Some instinct hidden from deep within rose to the surface. She gritted her teeth as her stomach tightened, and she groaned, her cheeks hollowing in and out. Her eyes squeezed shut.

The urge passed and she fell to the floor once more. Her eyes opened once more, staring into the crack underneath the door. The chilly air blew into her eyes, along with grit and dust.

Blinking rapidly, she tried to water out the dirt when another urge came upon her, this one fiercer than the last time. She gritted her teeth once again, eyes squeezed shut, feeling her body tense and tighten, using every ounce of her strength.

When it left, she sank back onto the floor, and gazed up at the ceiling.

The nightmare of being alone... it was coming true.

Here she was, lying on the floor, about to give birth and no one was there.

No one to hold her hand. No one to wipe her brow. No one to help her bring her child into the world. All alone.

*If I can just get to the door...*

Weakly, she rolled to her side and looked once more at the crack under the door. She squinted her eyes against the bright light and the slight flurry of snowflakes billowing inside the room when she saw the light dim.

Surprise took hold of her and she watched as the beam grew dimmer. Was it the sun hiding behind clouds? No, this was different.

She stared again as the darkness under the crack of the door neared. Her heart leapt into her chest when she saw the darkness divide.

For a moment, her mind drew a blank. Why would the darkness part in such a way?

Then comprehension dawned upon her.

Feet! A pair of feet at the door!

A thunderous knock shattered the loneliness that filled the house with its deafening roar.

"Hello?"

The door muffled the sound of the voice. She couldn't tell it if was male or female, friend or foe, but she didn't care. God had answered her prayer.

She wouldn't be alone.

The urge came upon her again. She lifted her legs and with a strangled cry of pain, she shouted. "Come in! Oh please! Come in!"

⁂

Wolfe Laingsburg peered around the door. The ready smile on his face froze when he glanced down to see a Negro woman writhing in pain on the floor.

"Oh please, help me!"

For a moment, he stood there in the cold doorway, stunned. Then, when another cry erupted from the woman's lips, he jolted himself into action, shutting the door. He threw his carrying case and satchel on the floor and fell to his knees besides the woman.

Next to this tiny thing, he felt like a giant bear.

Taking in her thrashing figure, he saw blood staining the front of her skirt and the hem.

Some monster had attacked her!

"Who did this to you?" He jumped to his feet. "Who did it?"

The woman's voice, hoarse and wispy, sounded from behind him. "What?"

His fingers flexed with the need to harm. "Who hurt you? Are they still in the house?"

Without waiting for an answer, he dodged about the place, crashing into the first door he saw and yanking it open.

Looking into the well-kept kitchen with its wood-burning stove, oak furniture, and empty sink, nothing was amiss in that place.

Running out of there, he dashed into another room, seeing it was a bedroom, with a four-poster bed and clean sheets. He went further in, jerking open a door to reveal a closet stuffed with garments.

No one there.

"Please come back!"

He ran out of the room and fell back to his knees besides her. "Who did this to you?"

A burgeoning rage built up inside. He'd rip the assailant from limb to limb. How could anyone hurt a—

"Don't be frightened. Tell me, who did this?"

Her eyebrows squished together. "What are you talking about?"

"You're bleeding and in pain. Who hurt you? Who left you here in this agony?"

He bent his head but drew back when her eyes crossed. Maybe he was too close.

"I will find the person who did this to you."

She shook her head. "No, you don't understand. I wasn't attacked or anything like that."

He blinked. "But... but..."

She cried out and he gushed, "What can I do? What is wrong?"

The woman panted, her head falling back. The cords of her slender throat strained against her skin.

"My child is coming," she eked out hoarsely.

A cold wave crashed onto his body. Wolfe gulped as his eyes bulged in his head. "I beg your pardon?"

"My child... is coming." She groaned.

Slowly, his gaze drifted downward to see the swell of her stomach pressed against her clothes. This time, all the warmth of his body drained from him.

"My child—"

"Yes, yes," he said, trying to keep himself from screaming like a young girl. "I heard you say that. I'm not sure what that has to do with me."

Her brown eyes glistened. "Please, please don't leave me alone. I couldn't bear it."

Something stabbed his heart and lodged itself there at the pleading look in her eyes.

"But I—"

"I can feel—"

She sobbed and instinctively his hand went out. The woman grabbed hold of it and squeezed. Her grip was so tight he had the wild notion she would crush his bones. Despite that he let her, acting on a strange instinct to give this woman whatever it was she needed.

When the moment passed, she fell back to the floor, her chest heaving. "Please, you have to help me."

"Of course," he replied. "If you tell me where she is, I can go get the midwife and—"

"No, there's no time." She gasped and clamped on his arm. "I think the baby is coming right now."

A strange laugh erupted from Wolfe's mouth. "That can't be."

She yelled and her legs parted under the drape of her skirt. With a sickening sense of dread, he saw the way the urge went through her, saw the clenched teeth, the sweating brow.

Underneath it all, he saw the fear. The wild, leaping fear that underpinned everything else.

"I don't know what to do," she panted. "The babe's coming now."

Wolfe gulped. "The only babe I've seen exiting a mother's womb is the one with hooves."

The woman gave a startled, raspy laugh. "Oh, dear. I didn't expect that."

The tightness in his chest eased at the fleeting smile on her face.

She groaned once more as the urge came again, holding her still like a statue. "Sir, please. I don't want to be alone."

Wolfe stared at the woman as she became the focal point of the world. Nothing else existed but her sweat-stained face, her bloodied and soiled gown, her clenching fingers, and her plea.

What was he supposed to do? It was highly improper for a man to be present at a birthing. Furthermore, this woman, whoever she was, wasn't his wife.

He had come to Last Chance to *meet* his potential bride, a Negro widow who already had a child and was looking to have a father for it. When he'd knocked on the door after losing his way, he'd only been about to ask for directions.

How could he be in this place like this? What help had he to give?

But... how could he leave her all alone, even in this?

"Miss, I'm a praying man and before I do anything, I'm going to pray."

"Oh no," the woman groaned, rolling her eyes. "The babe will have turned a year old by the time you finish praying."

Wolfe drew back. "Why would you say that?"

"Whenever Pastor Collins prays, he prays as if he and God are on a long train ride in an empty car."

He swallowed back a laugh and said instead. "I promise, I won't pray that long." Clasping her small hands into his own, he bowed his head and said in succinct words, "Lord, we don't know what we're doing but you do. Help me help this woman and bring her child safely into the world. In Jesus's name, Amen."

When his eyes opened, he saw she had a strange look in her eyes, but when he would have questioned her, the urge came again, harder, and stronger than before.

"Oh no! I think the babe's coming," she cried out.

Her eyes squeezed shut as she gritted, the vein along the side of her head visible against the delicate skin of her temple. In an odd way, he ached for her. In this moment, he wished he could take the pain away from her. But he couldn't.

All he could do was be there by her side.

Her body went limp, and he saw her skin blanch of color. There was no way he was going to let the woman give birth to a child on a dusty floor. For a swift moment, he thought about his potential bride. Would that woman have as much strength as this one? Although he had seen the terror in her eyes when he entered, she was prepared to bring her child into the world.

A woman of strength.

He had been taught to protect the fairer sex at all costs. To never raise a voice or a hand. Perhaps he'd been given a misconception about Adam's rib. This woman's tenacity he admired in more ways than one.

Praying silently and carefully as he could, he swept his arms under her delicate body. Lifting her up, he stared down at her weak, fluttering lashes and then, with a sure stride, carried her into the bedroom and kicked the door closed behind them.

# **Chapter Two**

"I can't believe you, Altar! Why didn't you listen to me when I offered to stay? If you weren't so stubborn. If it wasn't for the fact I was coming to check on you anyway, you could have—"

Altar barely heard Heather's scolding above the massive weariness that washed through her body and seeped into her bones. She'd never felt so tired in her life. No one had ever told her that giving birth would be so painful and exhausting. That she would be forced to call upon a will she didn't know she had. Faced with a fear of everything and come out with the most precious jewels she'd ever seen in her life.

"And I should have known that only you would give birth to twins by yourself," Heather muttered, but her blue eyes gazed with fondness and awe on the two wrinkly children nestled in clean clothes by her side.

Twin boys.

"I still can't believe it," she breathed out. "Twins."

Heather bent and traced a light finger on the cusps of a tiny ear. "They're so beautiful." A pucker appeared between her brows. "Didn't you say your mother was a twin?"

Slowly, Altar nodded. "She was. My aunt died when I was a young girl."

Despite the joy coursing through her, she felt a little cloud of sadness come over her as she thought about her aunt. With a shake of her head, Altar thrust the thought out of her mind. This was a moment for rejoicing.

"Do you need me to give you any more advice about the feedings?"

Altar glanced down at her sons suckling on her breasts. Before their birth, she wasn't sure if she could love one child. She had told Elbert many times before that she did not want to be a mother. When it happened, she'd been upset with her husband and God. Over time, she grew used to the idea but even then, a thousand thoughts of regret had assaulted her.

Now, as she stared down at the two heads of black silky hair, noted the closed, dark-veined eyelids, and saw the tiny cherubic mouths taking their nourishment, a love like nothing she had ever experienced flooded her whole being.

"No, I'll be fine."

Heather gave a nod and then picked up the soiled bedding and laundry, wrapping them into a big ball. "I must say, that man who opened the door startled me for a few moments."

"Did he?" Altar asked.

"Yes, only because he's so big. I've seen trees shorter than him."

Altar let loose a light, weak chuckle, but she couldn't disagree with Heather's assessment. Through the pain of the birthing, she'd only caught impressions of the Negro man. Tall, and roped with muscles from what she could see. He had a short crop of hair on his head and a thick beard that covered the lower half of his face nicely. That was the most she could remember.

"He was very kind to me."

Kind didn't begin to describe what he was to her. An answer to prayer was more likely. Whenever this Wolfe Laingsburg arrived in Last Chance, she hoped that he exuded the same qualities this man had.

"I'm sure," Heather agreed absently as she straightened around the room.

"Although we had no idea what we were doing, together, we were able to bring my sons into the world."

A sudden stillness came over Heather. "What did you say?"

"He helped me. Heather, why are you looking like that?"

The woman's face paled. "Altar, please tell me this is a jest of some kind."

"Why are you saying that?"

Heather placed the ball of laundry into the basket. "This is not good, Altar. Not good at all."

"Whatever do you mean?"

Her mouth opened to speak when a knock sounded. With a sigh, Heather went to the door and cracked it open. Although she couldn't see the man who had helped her, Altar heard his deep, rich voice say, "May I come in now?"

"I'm afraid not, sir. The children are nursing and she's certainly exhausted and—"

"Oh, do stop, Heather," Altar interjected weakly. True, she was weary and true, she could do with a bout of uninterrupted sleep, but she couldn't let another second go by without thanking the man who had helped her at the lowest moment in her life. "At the risk of sounding wanton, there is no need for propriety. He's already seen—"

Heather's face flamed with color. "Yes, yes, Altar. But I am here now, and we must adhere to certain dictates of society."

"Let him in," Altar insisted, feeling her eyes droop just as one of the children's mouths unlatched from her. "I want to thank him properly."

With a frown on her head, Heather made a gesture to the waiting man and then shut the door. "Altar, far be it from me to say this, but you cannot allow that man in here again."

"Why not?"

Carefully, Heather took the first babe, and lifted him into her arms. Altar longed to care for him herself, but she was very weak.

Heather cooed to the babe as she wiped his face and rubbed his back. "It isn't done. I can't believe you allowed him to—to—"

"There was no one else, Heather," Altar interjected with a sigh. "I was so alone."

A hard knot entered her throat. Her other son, still nestled to her breast, whimpered as if he were sensing her emotion. With a limp but loving hand, she smoothed her fingers across his face. "Mother and Daddy are... gone now. I don't know when they'll be back."

"What about your—"

Altar's head jerked away from her son's and she narrowed her eyes. "Don't even mention that name."

Heather's blue eyes filled with compassion. "If you ever want to talk about it—"

"You were saying?" Altar refused to let *that* name be spoken in her presence.

The midwife's eyes gleamed but she went on. "This man is not your husband, Altar. The fact that he has become... privy to that part of you reserved for your groom, it will cause a problem. Particularly with Pastor Collins. He's not going to like this at all."

"We'll worry about it when it's time. Please, let him in."

Shaking her head, Heather gave the babe in her arms to Altar and switched to the other child. He whimpered for a moment, and Altar's heart twinged at the sound. This one seemed to want to be closer to her than the other. The first one was already falling asleep on her chest.

Heather smoothed her hand over the tiny body. Altar, watching the gentle movements, said unthinkingly, "It's a shame you don't have children. You would make a wonderful mother."

The midwife's face flushed red. Altar let out a groan. Once again, she'd insulted this kind woman. "Please forgive me. I didn't mean to be insensitive."

Another wobbly smile came to Heather's face. "Yes, well..."

The words trailed off. Heather turned her attention to the babe and another brief silence settled between them. Altar covered herself sufficiently and then said, "Please, let him in."

Giving her a final glance, Heather went over to the door and opened it. "You can come in now."

"Thank you."

Heather moved back to let the man in. Altar's eyes lifted way up into the air, seeing for the first time just how large and towering the man was. He had to be almost seven feet tall.

"How are you doing?" he asked, his dark eyes assessing and oddly inscrutable.

"Exhausted," she answered. "But I'll feel better if I can have the honor of knowing the name of the man who came to my rescue."

Wolfe listened to the murmurings of the women behind the door. Although he couldn't make out their words, he could hear the low and high notes likes strains of music.

He paced away from the door, rubbing the back of his neck as he thought about the events of the past hour or so.

He now knew the reason why men should not be present in the birthing room. No man could stand by and watch a woman he loved go through that ordeal and not wish that the Lord Almighty could use his body in some way to take away her pain.

Wolfe hadn't even known the woman, much less loved her, and the sight of her straining to bring her children into the world gave him the same desire.

As a former steel driver, he knew what it meant to be strong. Or so he had thought. Now, he found himself rethinking what it meant to have strength. That woman had shown more tenaciousness than anything he'd ever experienced before in his life, including when—

The door opened and the midwife stepped back to allow him entrance. Wolfe took a moment to study the woman. She looked much different with her hair straightened, dressed in fresh clothes, and her face void of the lines of pain that had tautened her features. Her skin had a smooth, russet brown hue along with a square chin. Her brown eyes stared into his wearily, but still held an alert light within their depths.

"How are you doing?"

She gave a little tilt of her head. "Exhausted. But I'll feel better if I can have the honor of knowing the name of the man who came to my rescue."

Wolfe blinked. "I never introduced myself," he said in a disbelieving voice. "Nor did I ever receive your name."

"We were occupied by more pressing matters. Two in fact," the woman quipped.

"That's true. Well, my name is Wolfe Laingsburg."

The woman's eyes widened greatly. "Wolfe Laingsburg?"

"That's correct," he drew out, wondering why she looked so shocked.

"I-I'm Altar. Altar Pennington."

He took a step forward. "Altar Pennington. I answered your letter for—"

Mrs. Pennington's mouth gaped open. "I thought you weren't going to be here until sometime next month. That's what you stated in your letter."

Wolfe shook his head. "I was, but... circumstances led me to change my mind and I decided to come earlier than expected." His eyes drifted to the sleeping baby on her chest and then to the one being held by the midwife. "I thought you said you already had a child."

"I thought the babe would have come before your arrival."

They stared at each other. This was much more than coincidence. Had God led him here?

"How did you know I lived here?" Mrs. Pennington asked after a moment.

"I didn't," he answered as he came around the bed. "I had stopped by this house because I was lost."

"Incredible." Mrs. Pennington shook her head once more. "And you were the one who helped me."

"I take it that Mr. Laingsburg answered your advertisement, Altar?"

Wolfe had forgotten that the midwife was there. Despite her help, he wanted the woman out of there. Altar and he needed to talk without anyone being privy to their conversation.

"That's correct." Mrs. Pennington's eyes drooped again. "Heather, Mr. Laingsburg, I'm very tired. I think I am going to sleep for now. My sons..."

"They are both asleep and I'll look after them," the midwife—Heather—promised. "I'll come back and get the other one."

"No," Wolfe said as he bent down. "I'll take the other one."

Mrs. Pennington lifted her gaze to him, her brown eyes questioning. His large broad fingers patted her arm. He noted the delicateness of her slender limbs. With a careless exercise of strength, he could snap her arm in two. And yet, she'd nearly crushed the fingers in his hand during the birthing.

"I swear, I won't do anything to harm him."

"You know something, Mr. Laingsburg? I believe you."

His heart hammered in his chest as his big, dark paws picked up the small child nestled against his mother. He wasn't used to holding small, fragile things in a general sense. He'd never held a newborn babe. But he watched the way the midwife held the one in her hands, and he mimicked her. When he straightened to his full height, he caught the babe close to his chest.

Once more, his gaze strayed to Mrs. Pennington. She gave a sigh, of relief or fear, it was impossible to know because her body slumped, and he could see she'd fallen asleep.

"Come, Mr. Laingsburg. Bring him here. The basket is out here for now."

He took a minute step, trying to swallow the lump in his throat as he realized the enormity of his task.

Walking to the door without dropping the baby.

A cold sweat beaded his body like rain. Oh, dear Lord! Why did he think he could do this? Mrs. Pennington trusted him to be careful with her child. What if he fell? What if he tripped or slipped or—

"Just one step at a time, Mr. Laingsburg," the midwife cooed.

Her soft voice made it through the whirlwind that had enclosed his brain. "Just one step and then the next."

For all her disapproval of his being there, her blue eyes filled with sympathy at his dilemma. He saw that she'd already put the child down in the basket and was waiting by the door.

"Unless you want me to take him for you?"

Her offer titillated him for a moment, but he shook his head. "No. I told Mrs. Pennington that I would let nothing happen to him and I won't. I can do this."

Taking in a deep breath, he said a quick prayer. He went across the room, focused on the midwife as if she were an angel of light.

In this case, she was!

When she closed the door behind him, she gestured for him to take a seat in the small parlor room he had discovered while he waited as she'd attended to Mrs. Pennington earlier. The fire blazed heartily, and the basket was far enough away but still near to enjoy the warmth.

"I'll take him."

"I can do it, Miss—"

"Mrs. Barnes," she answered with a somewhat fierce, defiant tone. He had the strangest notion that she was speaking more to herself than to him. "Please, I'll take the baby."

He handed the sleeping babe over and watched as the midwife settled him next to his brother, bundling the babe snug.

His legs weakened and he collapsed onto a chair. "Oh, dear Lord. That was probably the hardest thing I've ever done in my life."

"In my work, I have found babies are weaker than we know and stronger than we can grasp. It's a wonder they survive until they are grown." She became brisk. "Mr. Laingsburg, I must insist that you leave immediately. Although I understand that you are responding to the advertisement we placed in the newspapers, surely it isn't proper for you to be here."

Wolfe wiped the sweat from his brow. "Why not?"

"Are you going to marry Mrs. Pennington?"

He glanced away from the hard blue eyes. "I'm sure that is something I will discuss with Mrs. Pennington."

The woman gave a huff. "Very well. I can't make you leave here for propriety's sake, but Altar is my friend. I will be back to check on her for the next several days."

"I should hope so."

"Look, Mr. Laingsburg, there's a hotel on Main and First. You can stay there for the time being. It's not too far from this house and you can visit with Altar every day if you wish."

Wolfe could see she wanted to see the back of him. "Why do you want me to leave so badly, Mrs. Barnes?"

Her even, white teeth kneaded the right side of her lower lip. "New men are arriving in town all the time because of the advertisement. We had no idea that we would be inviting unsavory elements into our midst. If it wasn't for Pastor Collins' insistence..."

She blew out a breath. Reaching over, she placed her pale hand against his. "Mr. Laingsburg. I don't believe you are an unscrupulous man. No man who did what you did could be that. It's Pastor Collins who I am worried about."

"You've mentioned him several times now, Mrs. Barnes. Is he a hard man? An evil one?"

She snorted. "No, Pastor Collins isn't evil. He's a busybody as the saying goes. He sticks his nose into everyone's business and judges all based on his view of the way things should be."

"Then why are you worried?"

She drew back and stared pensively at the fire. "I'm afraid he's going to make trouble for you. One way or another."

# **Chapter Three**

Gentle snowflakes sparkled in the weak sunshine outside the kitchen window. As he stared at them, Wolfe knew he should have left three days ago.

He had the feeling wild horses wouldn't be able to drag him away.

"It's too soon to think like that," he said out loud as he pulled his attention away from the scenery outside and continued to prepare breakfast for himself and Altar, while she nursed the babies in her bedroom. "Let's just live for today."

Thankful for the cooking lessons his mother made him participate in as a child, he easily scrambled eggs, fried three rashers of bacon, and a stack of flapjacks. It wasn't the most elegant meal, but it was filling. From what Altar had told him, they were blessed to have what they did.

Mrs. Barnes came over several times in the past three days. Although he suspected that she was helping Altar recover from the birthing, he also sensed she was keeping an eye on him.

After all, he hadn't left the house since he poked his head in the door to ask for directions. He'd taken to sleeping in a small study room, much smaller than the parlor, with a tiny little couch not big enough for a mouse. Yet, it gave them both some element of decency.

"Breakfast is almost ready," he called out.

"Thank you," he heard the faint voice respond back.

Taking plates and silverware from the cupboard, he loaded them with food. He never thought he'd be in a place like this. Not the location. Last Chance was a robust community despite the heavy loss of men and animals in the blizzards that had devastated the town.

No, not the location but this place in his life.

After the incident that happened a few months ago, he had found himself swirling down a dark tunnel, unable to find light in any way. The betrayal he suffered at the hands of a person who he would have given his life for had taken its toll. Not a drinking man or a man who had participated in hard living, he had no way to numb his sorrow.

Work had once been his only refuge. Now that was gone. He'd saved his earnings over the years, in addition to the monies he'd received from his mother upon her death, so he did have sufficient funds to carry him through.

It wasn't until he had read the advertisement in the newspaper that he found a spark ignite within him. His life as a steel driver was over. Maybe he could find a wife and settle down like most men did.

How did a man settle down when he spent most of his life working? Hard labor, prize fighting, or using some other method to show off his strength. That had been his life until this year.

He'd slept on the idea that night and when he'd awakened, he knew he had nothing else to lose. Swiftly, before he could change his mind, he wrote a response and sent it to the post office along with a prayer.

Now, here he stood, feeling something other than despair. Other than betrayal.

He was starting to feel like himself again.

Well, as much as he could feel like his old self.

As he reached for the plates, his right hand started to shake. Grimly, he fisted it, trying to still its trembling. He glared at it, desperate to will away the weakness.

Another reminder of that terrible betrayal.

Although it lasted for mere seconds, it seemed an age had gone by before he had control of his hand again.

Balancing the plates on both hands, he placed them on a tray he found and carried them into the bedroom.

Altar lay against the pillows, her dark face serene and impersonal. Her brown-eyed gaze met his as he entered. The boys were taking their nourishment. He turned his head away, but in all honesty, he wasn't disturbed by the improperness of the situation.

He should be, but he wasn't.

After all, he had seen her in less, but she still had his respect. If they were to marry, he would be privy to such things in the future.

Or would he?

"Why are you scowling?"

He set the tray on the small table near the bed and sat next to her in the chair he brought into the bedroom. They both would have preferred to eat in the kitchen. Though she was on the mend, she was still very weak. Wolfe refused to let propriety stop him from taking care of her. If they had to eat and talk in the bedroom while she nursed her sons, so be it.

"I wasn't aware that I was doing that."

"You were. Not in a fierce manner, but you do seem to be in deep thought."

He picked up his plate and said a quick prayer. After which, he started to eat. "I was thinking of our situation, Altar. We've not really had a chance to speak about it."

Her brown eyes drifted down, revealing her long lashes. "I see."

"I know you're still healing and all, but I feel as if we soon need to discuss this thing between us."

The silence rested between them, but it wasn't unpleasant. In fact, as he sat and ate, he couldn't think of anything more peaceful than this moment. The babes nestled against their mother in an age-old scene of contentment.

"We do need to discuss things. I am grateful that you haven't pushed the issue so far, Wolfe."

"I never would. But I know that Mrs. Barnes keeps coming here and she looks a bit fiercer each time."

Altar's brown lips lifted in a half smile. "She's a spitfire, all right. I think she's reined in her temper somewhat because of my condition. She's worried about what Pastor Collins would say."

"This man... why does he have such influence over the people?"

She gave a nonchalant shrug. "He's our preacher. A man of God. They always have influence over the people."

"But to force you women to choose a new spouse so soon after your husbands passed. Surely that decision to remarry should be up to each woman."

"It should be," Altar answered in a drawn-out voice. "But I think Pastor Collins thinks he is doing what is best for the town. When news of the deaths came, I think all he saw was a bunch of women without the protection of their men."

Thinking of the way he found her when he came three days ago, he said, "I read about the blizzards in the paper. What was it like for you?"

She lifted her gaze to his. "I was stuck in the schoolhouse for days with some of the children and a couple of the other women. The temperature kept dropping faster and faster. Getting colder almost by the minute. Water froze on the roof. Snow blanketed everything."

Her eyes lost focus. "I remember when Heather went out to check on the pump. She came back in nearly frozen. The children were frightened, and everyone was forced to wait. I sang to try to ease the young one's fears, all the while wishing someone would ease my own.

"Even then, Wolfe, as horrible as those days were, and the days that followed, whenever I look back, I was so thankful that I wasn't alone. The day you came, I thought for sure that I would be alone. I dislike being alone."

Her voice had taken on a husky melodious sound. It enchanted him. "Why?"

Those brown eyes looked away. "I have my reasons."

Wolfe knew not to push any further. He finished his breakfast and set the empty plate back on the tray. "Well, now that you have these fellas, you won't have to worry about that ever again."

Her head turned sharply in his direction. Those brown eyes, which had looked so cool and detached, warmed like a cup of hot tea. "You're right. With these two, I'll never be alone again." She looked down at the babes who were finished taking their nourishment. "Thank you for telling me that."

Wolfe shrugged. "Let me take the first one here."

He deliberately averted his eyes to give her a chance to gather herself together and turned back to pick up the first one to help with his burping.

"Oh, you'll need a rag in case he—"

"Don't worry about it none. He's already gotten sick on me and let loose a stream on me when I changed his nappy. What's one more?"

Altar laughed and her entire face brightened. Wolfe stared as he took the boy and placed him on his shoulder, careful to make sure his chin rested on the top as he rubbed his back. She was really a beautiful woman.

"Yes, but I don't have the strength to do laundry right now. Or cleaning. Or mending, or anything else. But in a town like this, some of the women will be coming by and helping out until I can get back to my regular duties."

She took her other son and began to rub his back. Her eyes closed in bliss.

"Have you thought of names for them yet?"

"I have."

"What are they?"

She nodded in his direction. "Since he's the youngest, I'm naming him Alpha. Since this one here is the oldest, I'm naming him Omega."

Wolfe paused in his slight bouncing of the child. "I beg your pardon?"

"That's right. He's Omega and that one is Alpha."

"Why Alpha and Omega? And why switch them around that way?"

"The last shall be first and the first shall be last."

Wolfe blinked. There were worse names. He just couldn't think of any. It was clear that rock throwing from bullies would be in his sons' futures.

His sons? Had he really thought that?

The sound of the door opening made them both turn their heads. Wolfe, figuring it was Mrs. Barnes, wasn't alarmed. Until he heard her high voice arguing with another high voice.

"You can't go in there," he heard Mrs. Barnes say clearly.

A thunder of footsteps sounded on the floor. A wimpish man with pale skin, lank hair, and a weak chin, dressed like a parson, centered himself in the doorway. His eyes, wide in disbelief and horror, gazed back and forth between Wolfe and Altar. His voice shook as he said, "So it's true. You've been living in sin, Altar."

Altar couldn't tear her eyes away from the sight of the preacher in her doorway. Heather stood behind the man who blocked her entry, lifting her shoulders helplessly.

"I tried to stop him, Altar," Heather said. "Believe me, I did."

Pastor Collins puffed his chest out. Altar bit back a groan. Whenever he did that, she knew he would begin to pontificate in a sonorous voice.

"How did he find out?"

Heather groaned. "Lisa. Lisa Speciale."

Altar groaned. The older woman had come over yesterday and must have told the preacher. Not in a malicious way, but as one would beloved children. She'd already agreed to look after them.

"Thanks be to the Almighty God, the Ruler of the World, and the Hope of the Saints that Mrs. Barnes could not prevent me from overtaking the wily hands of the devil from stamping out sin that has gathered in this house."

Wolfe's mouth fell open. "What did he say?"

The preacher snorted in derision as he came further into the room, his hat clutched in his hands as if it were imbuing him with holy power. "I'm not surprised that a man such as yourself wouldn't begin to comprehend the words of the Almighty. You, sir, I shall take to task."

Before Wolfe could say anything, and judging by the look in his eyes Altar sensed he was at a loss for words, Pastor Collins came to the foot of the bed. "Altar Pennington, why have you allowed your grief at the death of your husband to put your immortal soul in jeopardy?"

She tried to speak, but Omega made a mewling sound, and she checked on him. His tiny eyes were scrunched. Was he picking up on the moods in the room?

"Even the child knows, Altar. What would your dear mother, Permelia, may God give that sainted woman grace, and your father Horace, may God give him the strength to carry on in his works, say if they saw you like this?"

*They'd probably slam the door in your face before they'd scold me.*

Permelia and Horace had never liked the man.

"Pastor Collins, please understand. I am not living in sin with Mr. Laingsburg."

"Altar, I was willing to give you the illustrious benefit of my name, to spare you from living a life of sin. And yet, you've thrown away my offer of protection and have taken up with harlot ways."

"You are treading on dangerous ground, preacher. I suggest you turn around and leave the way you came." Wolfe's voice had deepened in a way she'd not heard before.

Altar sent a startled glance in Heather's direction. The midwife correctly interpreted her look as she pushed past the preacher and went over to Wolfe, who gave Alpha to her. Not that Altar didn't trust him... but she didn't trust him. Not when his voice and demeanor had so drastically changed.

For the past three days, Wolfe had been nothing but kind, courteous, and respectful. He'd cooked all the meals, helped her adjust her position in the bed when she needed to move, changed the boys' nappies, and rocked the children to sleep in a rocking chair her father had made for her mother years ago. If it weren't for the fact that they weren't married, she would have believed they were married.

His initial uneasiness with handling her sons had eased away, showing a man of layers. It seemed at odds with his giant, muscular form, suited for the steel driving work he told her he once did.

But his temperament with the preacher gave her pause. What sort of man *was* Wolfe Laingsburg? For all of Pastor Collins' faults, maybe he was right to show some wariness towards him.

Or was she simply using that as an excuse? But an excuse for what?

"Mr. Laingsburg, is it?" The preacher strutted over to where Wolfe stood and stared up at him. Most men would have approached with caution.

Pastor Collins' sense of self-importance stood taller than Wolfe.

"Yes, my name is Mr. Laingsburg."

"Now see here, Mr. Laingsburg. I am charged with this woman's soul. I won't be intimidated, especially as you seem bent on sending her soul straight to the fiery pits of hell."

"Pastor Collins, please listen to me."

He held up his hand. "No, Altar. You listen to me, both of you. Are you and Mr. Laingsburg married?"

"No, but—"

The preacher wagged his finger. "No, I am the one asking questions. Has not Mr. Laingsburg stayed in this house for the past few days?"

"Yes, but—"

"Alone with you?"

She swallowed and her eyes shifted to Wolfe. "Y-yes, Pastor Collins."

"Did you seek the attendance of a chaperone while—"

"Now you stop it right there, Pastor Collins."

Wolfe took a step closer to the man, his dark eyes hard. "When I came here, Mrs. Pennington was lying on the floor of this house, writhing in pain and bleeding, trying to bring her children into the world. There was no one to assist her but me. Tell me, Pastor Collins, should I have left her lying on the floor? For propriety's sake?"

Altar's head started to shake. Wolfe, he was going too far. "Wolfe, please!"

"Should I have left her lying there in her own waste? Maybe she should have borne her sons on the floor instead of in my arms so I could protect them."

Oh no!

Pastor Collins's face took on a hue like soured cream. "My God in Heaven! Are you saying you were with Mrs. Pennington? You... you... acted in the stead of the midwife?"

The tone in the preacher's voice cut through Wolfe's anger. She could see the moment when his ire seeped away and he came to the dawning realization that he shouldn't have revealed his part in the birth of the twins.

A dubious look entered the preacher's eyes. "Are you a doctor, sir?"

The bulge in Wolfe's throat bobbed. "No, but—"

"A midwife, perhaps? I've heard there are men who possess the skill as well."

"No, I—"

He held up his hand. "There is no need to continue this discussion."

"Wait, I—"

"Why didn't you go for the midwife as soon as you saw her state?" Pastor Collins stepped forward. "Why did you take it upon yourself to perform a duty for which you are not trained or skilled nor capable of performing?"

"If I was her husband, you wouldn't be objecting to this at all."

"That's correct, Mr. Laingsburg, I wouldn't. A husband has certain rights of his wife. None of which you can claim."

"I saw—"

"You could have called another woman! I'm sure if you knocked on a few doors, any of the women would have come to Mrs. Pennington's aid."

Altar gaped as the preacher stabbed his finger in Wolfe's direction, righteous fury burning in his eyes. "You had no right to do what you did and take advantage of this woman."

"Pastor Collins, please, Wolfe, I mean, Mr. Laingsburg did not take advantage of me."

"I am a God-fearing man, Pastor Collins, I would never do such a thing."

The preacher snorted and walked back to the door. "And yet, here we are with evidence to the contrary."

Wolfe's nostrils flared.

Altar met Heather's wide blue eyes. For once, the midwife was speechless as everything spiraled quickly out of control. How had this happened? Was it only moments ago that she and Wolfe were sitting together, enjoying breakfast? Although she hadn't eaten hers, she enjoyed the time.

Now, her reputation was at risk.

At first, she found the preacher's interference meddlesome, but in hindsight, she could see things from his point of view. There was an awful rightness to his logic. Wolfe could have gone to anyone else to gain assistance. He could have hurried and searched for another woman, any woman, to come to her aid.

Why hadn't she thought of that herself?

*Because I was terrified of being alone when my child came.*

Her gaze shifted back to Wolfe; he stood, tension emanating from his body. Could she blame the man for doing what he did? He was there when she needed him.

But it was possible they could have handled the situation a lot differently.

"There is only one way to rectify this. One way alone."

"Oh? And what is that?" Altar asked, straightening her back. Would he tell her she'd have to leave town now?

"You must marry immediately. This day."

# **Chapter Four**

"You can't be serious about this," Wolfe exclaimed as the preacher turned to leave the room.

"Oh, Mr. Laingsburg, I am quite serious."

He stared down at the little man who stood before him with such affront and defiance. Why did little men like this wield so much power while big men like him were forced to do their bidding?

"You cannot make me marry Mrs. Pennington."

"Oh, can't I?" the little man sneered. "Let me be perfectly clear. If you and she do not marry this day, you and she will have to leave Last Chance."

Both the women interjected in shocked voices.

"Pastor Collins, please—!"

"Wait!"

"I don't believe you." Wolfe narrowed his eyes at the man. His fist clenched at his sides. It wasn't that he didn't want to marry Mrs. Pennington. The fact was that the decision was up to her. Though they had shared moments of great intimacy unrelated to the marriage bed, there still existed a chasm between them.

How well did anyone know anyone anyway? His mind drifted back to the incident months ago. He thought he knew that person well. Thought that he knew them outside and in. They had shared many moments of life together.

Then he was betrayed.

Yes, Altar Pennington seemed like a nice woman. But was it only a farce? A clever disguise to hide a different nature than the one she presented to the outside world. In the letter, she had stated she had a child, not that she was still carrying it. It seemed a small omission but with Pastor Collins threatening to force her away, he had to think of these things.

What about her reluctance to discuss their potential marriage? Why? There were a lot of things about this woman he did not know. The whole point of traveling to this town was to spend some time getting to know her.

To have that opportunity snatched away by the likes of the little man before him—!

"You can't send Mrs. Pennington and her children out of town, Pastor Collins."

"I can and I will," the man answered confidently. "Call me heartless, Mr. Laingsburg. Call me whatever it is you like, but Mrs. Pennington's mortal soul is in danger." He spread his arms out. "Sin sits at this house, licking its mouth as it waits to devour both of you."

"I have done nothing to be ashamed of, Pastor Collins. Neither has she. For goodness' sake, look at her." He gestured in Altar's direction. "Do you really believe she can perform wifely duties, or any duty of any kind, right now?"

"That doesn't matter. The good book says, '*Abstain from the appearance of evil*'."

"More than appearances, Pastor Collins! Any form of it, and I've not done anything of the like. And what can be evil about bringing a child into the world?"

"Nonetheless—"

"Should," Wolfe interjected in a tight voice, "a marriage between myself and Mrs. Pennington take place, it will be because we chose for that to happen, not you."

The preacher's face flushed red. "I am the shepherd of this flock, and I will protect it, even if I have to send a wayward sheep to the wolves in order to preserve its soul."

A hard, humorless laugh sounded out of Wolfe's mouth. "Jesus wouldn't send a sheep out to the wolves. He'd kill the wolf before He'd let anything happen to the sheep."

Pastor Collins opened his mouth and then paused. He stared at Wolfe with something bordering on surprise, but then he shrugged. "You may have something there, Mr. Laingsburg. I'll give you that. But I'm still going to do what I can to save both of your souls from damnation."

Without another word, Pastor Collins stomped out of the room.

"I'll talk to him," Mrs. Barnes said as she cradled Alpha in her arm. "I'll try to see if I can get him to change his mind."

Her gaze shifted back and forth between Altar and Wolfe. Although he could see she was concerned, he knew he had to speak with Altar alone.

They had much to discuss.

"Mrs. Barnes, Mrs. Pennington and I need some time to discuss... things. If you can see to her needs and then leave, I will greatly appreciate your kindness."

He tried to make the words come out as a request, but he could tell from the look in her eye, she knew he wasn't asking her.

Altar moved on the bed, holding Omega close to her. It was then that he noticed throughout the entire exchange that neither of the children had awakened or cried.

A small blessing.

Still looking at him, Mrs. Barnes asked, "Altar?"

Wolfe waited, realizing that he was acting in the same way the preacher had acted. Wearily, he dug his forefinger and thumb into his eye sockets. Demanding and commanding without any regard to her wants or desires. He sighed and sent another prayer to Heaven. Incoherent and full of half-framed pleas and wants, but a prayer, nonetheless.

Altar gave a slow nod. "He's right, Heather. We need to discuss things. Privately."

"What about the children?" she asked.

"We'll take care of them."

Wolfe felt a jolt go through him at the sound of those words.

Not 'I'll' but 'we'll'.

Clearing his throat, he went over to Mrs. Barnes and took Alpha in his arms again. The child simply moved to his other side, fast asleep. "Mrs. Barnes, can you get their basket for me?"

Before long, Wolfe sat in the parlor looking down at the sleeping children sharing the basket on the table. The crackling fire accompanied the silence in the parlor but did nothing to suppress the muffled voices of the women across the short hall. He could hear the faint sound of voices from behind the closed door and knew the women were talking. What they discussed, he didn't know, but he had a fair idea.

Their marriage.

Wolfe stretched his arms along the edge of the couch and his head fell back, looking up at the whitewashed ceiling.

What was he to do?

He thought back to Pastor Collins' words. He had to admit that not everything the parson said was wrong.

Therein lay the rub. The man was right and wrong in equal parts. He was wrong in thinking that Wolfe would ever willfully take advantage of a woman. Yet, he was right for his diatribe.

But that didn't matter either.

Could he sit still and let Pastor Collins throw them both out of the town?

Did he owe it to Altar to redeem her reputation even though this coercion wasn't the entrance into marriage that he wanted?

He lifted his head and stared at the two sleeping infants.

What about the children? In three short days, he had already become used to them. They didn't do much at all, just nurse and sleep most of the time. Unlike Altar, he couldn't tell them apart by simply looking. He had to check their ankles to see which one had a mole on the back of his heel. Hints of their personality, even in this short time frame, surfaced.

Omega, the eldest, whimpered whenever Altar winced or gasped from the lingering pains of childbirth. When he nursed, he tended to stay longer than his younger brother. Although Wolfe knew it was too early to tell, his instinct was that Omega had a strong protective stance for his mother.

Alpha was always the first to finish nursing. His body movements were jerkier, as if he were anxious to be about doing something else. His cries louder when he demanded his nourishment. Wolfe sensed the younger of the brothers had the more dynamic personality.

Those were his observations about the boys in three days. What would a lifetime look like? Could he really walk away from them?

Did he want to?

The door to the bedroom opened, and he stood and came to the entrance of the parlor. Mrs. Barnes bore a small roll of laundry. "Mr. Laingsburg, I'll be leaving now, but I'll be back in a couple of hours."

"Thank you."

Her blue-eyed gaze lingered for a moment, and then she said, "I hope you make the right decision."

As she was leaving, he stopped her by calling her name. "Yes?"

"What decision is that?"

She lifted her shoulders. "The one that is best for all of you."

When Wolfe entered the bedroom again carrying the basket with the children, Altar said, "Well, I can honestly say that I didn't expect to have to make a decision to marry you today."

His full lips twitched. "Neither did I. I simply wanted an understanding of where we were to start."

He set the basket on the table near the bed and then sat back down, drawing the chair close to the bed. This close, she saw tiny scars along his cheekbones and forehead. She glanced down at his hands. They looked big, hard, and calloused. Hands capable of causing great harm but held her sons' tiny bodies with such gentleness.

She found herself thinking of Elbert. He had rough hands as well, but they never seemed as kind as Wolfe's did.

Shaking her head to rid herself of the odd thought, she leaned forward so she could see her sons sleeping. Although the basket was big enough to house both for now, she knew they would have to have a crib made and soon.

They were the only two good things that Elbert ever gave her.

Wolfe's gaze drifted to the empty space on the table. "I guess Mrs. Barnes took the plate into the kitchen. Did you get a chance to eat anything?"

She shook her head.

He made as if to rise. "I can make you some more food," he offered.

She waved him back down. "I'll eat after we finish talking. I don't know how soon Pastor Collins will return, but I can assure you that once he does, he will be either performing a marriage or making sure that we leave Last Chance."

Wolfe rubbed the palm of his hands against his pants. "Before we go any further, I must apologize to you."

She opened her mouth to say the opposite when Wolfe shook his head. "No, Altar. That little man may be pompous, self-righteous, and bloated with his own self-worth. But he was not wrong to criticize my conduct of you. I should have sought out another woman to aid you. I shouldn't have taken liberties that were not mine. I truly meant no offense to you, and I hope you will forgive me."

"Then, I must apologize for taking advantage of your kindness. You did try to leave, but my fears overtook my sense. I didn't want to be alone, and I didn't care who it was that came through that door." A slight shiver went through her at the narrow escape. "Anyone, simply anyone could have come in and harmed me."

"But they didn't. I believe God allowed me to be the one because He knew I would never hurt you in any way."

Something that had been tense and wary eased away from her shoulders. She didn't even know it until it dissipated.

"Thank you."

"That begs the question, Altar. Where do we go from here?"

She picked at the edge of the blanket. "I guess we need to learn about each other, don't you think?"

"We should, although, from the way that Pastor Collins was going on, I don't think we'll have much time for courting."

She gave a wry, weak grin. "True. What does a woman like me need to know about a man like you?"

"Such as my family life?"

"That's a good place to start."

"My parents are dead. My father died from a disease that spread through the slave cabins at the plantation I grew up at. My mother died two years ago."

Altar's ears perked up. "You were a slave?"

"Of course," he frowned. "Weren't you?"

She shook her head. "No. The man who owned my mother and father gave them their freedom several years before the War. I was born free."

Wolfe looked surprised. "I've never known a Negro man or woman born free."

"There are many," she told him. "My parents are abolitionists. If I may say, you speak very well. How is that possible?

She listened as he told her how a white preacher had come by the plantation and given lessons to the children whenever he could. Wolfe went on to tell his story about how after Emancipation, he broke free of his bonds and took on work as soon as he could.

"I saw a notice in the newspaper about a labor company looking for workers, and I signed up. They were going to turn me away at first. When they saw how strong I was and how big, they hired me."

His eyes stared into the past, a strange sadness overshadowing his features. "What's wrong, Wolfe?"

He gave a slight shake, and his eyes lost their distance. "Nothing. I was just... remembering."

"Why did you stop working?"

He cleared his throat. "The machines came and they could work faster than a man. So my services were no longer needed. I went back home to the plantation where my mother stayed, and cared for her until she passed. After which I found odd jobs here and there until I saw the advertisement for grooms in the newspaper.

"That's who I am, Mrs. Pennington."

Why did she think there was more to his story than what he told her?

"Now, it's your turn. You said your parents are abolitionists. Do you have any siblings?"

She tensed up. Why wasn't she as willing to be forthcoming with her past as Wolfe had been with his?

But had he been forthcoming? Some part of her doubted that.

"I do," she said slowly. "I have a brother named Temple Sage."

"Temple Sage?" Wolfe's forehead wrinkled. "I thought you said he was your brother."

"He is in almost every sense of the word. He's really my cousin, but we grew up together and I consider him a brother."

"Any sisters?"

Her jaw clenched. "I don't want to talk about that."

Wolfe's dark eyes widened. "I see. I take it that you do have a sister, but that you are estranged."

Altar clipped out in a hard tone, "If I never see her again, it would be too soon."

"I see." He shifted in his chair. "Do you mind talking to me about your husband?"

"No," she said slowly. "Elbert and I married two years ago. He died in September."

Wolfe waited for her to say more, but she refused. Speaking about Elbert was almost the same as speaking about her sister. She had no wish to linger on them for too long.

"What did he do for a living?"

"He worked at a ranch a couple of hours ride outside of town. A few times a month he acted as an agent for a salt mine outside of town near Indian territory. Not too far from where he died. He supplied salt to various farms and businesses. Heather got her salt supply from him as well."

Those dark eyes of Wolfe's stared at her. He really was a handsome man, much better looking than Elbert had been. "So that's it?"

"What do you mean?"

"That's all you have to say about your husband? You married, he died, and he was a ranch hand and a salt agent?"

An invisible knot clogged in her throat. 'That's all I am going to say about him," she choked out through her tangled vocal cords.

Wolfe leaned forward. "Tell me, Altar. Did your husband ever hurt you?"

Hastily, she shook her head. "No, nothing like that, Wolfe."

"Then why—"

"Please." Her eyes closed. "My marriage to Elbert wasn't hard like some of the women in town. But it wasn't easy either. I tried to make the best of it, but I'll be frank. I was neither sad nor joyful when my husband died. It was simply the end of our marriage."

"Look at me."

Altar opened her eyes again to meet Wolfe's glittering gaze. "Yes?"

"Now that we know a little bit more about each other, I must ask you again." His voice dropped an octave. "Where do we go from here, Altar?"

A poignant silence settled over them. He was letting her know that the decision was hers to make.

Would things be different if she married Wolfe? He'd shown in many ways that he was different from Elbert. He knew how to cook for starters. Elbert couldn't start a fire with fire, much less boil water. Maybe marriage to this kind stranger would be something she could tolerate.

"I think we should consider marrying each other as Pastor Collins said."

Wolfe's mouth fell open. "You do?"

Taking in a deep breath, she said, "Yes, I do. My reasons for reaching out for a father for my sons still stands."

"Does that mean this is a marriage in name only? If so, I cannot agree to that. I'd like to have children of my own at some point. I can already tell you are an excellent mother and I'd be honored to make you the mother of my children."

Her face warmed. "I never... intended for this marriage to be in name only, Wolfe."

The tension released in his shoulders. "That's good to hear, Altar. When that happens, that will also be up to you. You will have to come to me."

"Wolfe!"

"Yes?"

"I thought that men... took charge of such things."

"I wouldn't know," he said enigmatically. She had little time to think on his words when the door to the house opened again. Pastor Collins stalked to the bedroom entry way.

"Now, have you decided to wash away the sins you have left upon this house and—"

Wolfe shook his head. "Pastor Collins, Altar, or rather, Mrs. Pennington, has agreed to marry me, sir."

The man's belligerent attitude changed in a blink of an eye. He became simpering, a smile wreathing his pale face. "Why, I am glad that the fear of the Holy God of the World, that Mighty Fortress and the Tower of Strength has opened your eyes to the error of your sinful ways."

He gestured with his hand. "Aren't you glad to hear that, Mrs. Fulton?"

No one answered

Pastor Collins's face became blank. "Mrs. Fulton? Mrs. Fulton? Where are you?"

"I'm here," Altar heard a timid voice say. It came from behind the door. "I don't want to be, but I'm here."

The preacher looked behind the door. "Well come out from behind there. You don't have to worry about their sinful acts any longer."

Ruby Fulton came from around the door. "Oh Altar, I'm so glad to hear about the twins. I was coming to see them, not..." She shrugged. "Not this."

"It's all right, Ruby. It's good to see you."

The woman gave a slight smile. "And you. What are the boys' names?"

"Ahem!" Pastor Collins interrupted in a loud voice. "Where is Mrs. Speciale?"

"I'm here," the older woman singsonged as she entered the house. "I just love weddings."

Altar looked down. She was dressed in a clean, but threadbare dress. Her husband-to-be wore stained pants and shirt.

"I'm glad you do, Mrs. Speciale."

Before Altar knew it, Pastor Collins began the ceremony to tie her and Wolfe Laingsburg in holy matrimony. "Dearly beloved..."

# **Chapter Five**

Omega and Alpha's cries penetrated the dark, blissful clouds of sleep like claps of thunder.

"Oh, dear God," Wolfe pleaded, groaning as he suppressed the urge to whimper as he forced himself awake for the third time that night. "Please let the boys fall to sleep. I'm so tired."

Sitting up from the tiny couch, he rubbed his eye sockets with his fists. He could hear the movements of Altar in the other room, her soft murmurings at contrast with the screeching the boys were doing.

One week had gone by since they married. In that short time, the boys went from being mostly concerned with nursing, filling nappies, and sleeping to screeching and crying at all hours of the day. The gentle, peaceful babies he'd met had turned into churlish wolf cubs.

Wolfe laughed despite his tiredness. Cubs, indeed!

Pushing himself off the couch, he went out the door and into Altar's bedroom.

He thought back to that first night. At first, he tried to wait until she finished before going into her bedroom to help. Although they were married now, sanctioned by God *and* Pastor Collins, he wanted to respect her privacy. The second night after they wed, she called him to help her get positioned, as one of the pillows she used to balance her arms as she fed the boys had fallen. In his haste to avert his eyes from the sight of her exposed flesh, he almost knocked the candle over.

Altar had sighed in an exasperated way. "Wolfe, I would rather you see me like this than you burn down the house trying to be respectful."

What could he have said to that?

Now, as he stood for a few seconds in the doorway, a single tongue of flame flared in the darkness, the match's light flowing softly over his wife's night-gowned form. She bent slightly to light the wick of the candle and the glow of firelight danced over her face.

For a moment, Wolfe couldn't tear his gaze away. A strange lurch surged in his chest as he followed the trail of light over her features. Did her eyebrows always have that long dramatic arch? Did her skin always have such a smooth, nearly flawless texture? Had her hair always been that thick?

It was as if he was seeing her for the first time.

Which was strange.

He cleared a suddenly dry throat and went further into the room and over to the basket where the boys' cries increased by the minute.

"You would think they were being whipped the way they're carrying on," he remarked as he picked up Alpha, wincing as the baby's shrill cry pierced his ears. "Alpha," he spoke in soft tones to the child, "you know your mother is going to feed you momentarily. Must you make so much noise, my little cub?"

Glancing down at Omega, who had quieted somewhat now that his brother wasn't there to egg him on, Wolfe shook his head in mock disappointment. "And you, Omega, you're the eldest. Aren't you supposed to tell him what to do?"

"I can see that Alpha will be the one to cause our hairs to gray much sooner."

Wolfe turned to see that Altar had gotten back into the bed, the pillows under her arms and positioned just so for ease. "All right, Wolfe. Bring His Majesty to me."

Alpha continued to yell as Wolfe walked over to where his wife lay. Carefully, he bent and handed the child to her, making sure she had a grip on him before letting go. Her hand moved to unbutton her gown and he swiftly turned back to pick up Omega.

His youngest son's cries stopped as if a cork had been shoved in his mouth.

"Peace, at last." Altar sighed.

Picking up Omega, he tutted softly at the babe who had stopped crying completely and made mewling noises. "I see that Omega is the patient one."

He went to the other side of the bed and placed a knee down to keep his balance as he went to give Altar the other child. Her knee went up, anchoring Alpha close as he guzzled while she took Omega.

"Hold him for me, will you?" she asked as her hand moved into the front of her nightgown. Wolfe kept his gaze fixed on his son as he waited.

"All right, I'm ready."

He handed Omega to Altar and soon, both boys were quiet.

Going over to the chair, he sat and leaned back, closing his eyes. Almost immediately, sleep lured him into its arms, but Altar's voice jolted him back.

"Wolfe, we are married now. I believe it is permissible for you to see me in this state."

He raised his head and looked at her and the sight of the boys against her.

"I know, but—"

"Yes?"

He dragged his fingers through his hair. "Perhaps Pastor Collin's words seeped further into my mind than I would have liked."

She gave a shake of her head. "What do you mean?"

"I keep thinking about what he said, and I feel guilty for what I did. Although I've apologized to you, I still feel as if I harmed you in some way."

"It's not you, Wolfe. It's him. He has a way of making you feel as if you can never be forgiven for the wrongs you've committed. That you have to pay penance for the rest of your life and even after death."

"Yes," he said with awe at her understanding. "That's exactly how I feel. I keep thinking over what I should have done, and it whirls around like a tornado."

"I know," she said quietly. "I had a similar experience with him."

"You have?"

She nodded. "I was going mad at the thoughts in my head. Finally, before my mother and father left with Temple, I went to their house and told them what had been troubling me. Talking to them, I realized what I had to do."

"And what was that?"

"I had to ask for forgiveness."

Wolfe tensed at the utterance of the word. "Forgiveness?"

"Yes. Forgiveness is difficult. Particularly when you are the one who has done wrong. I had the hardest time forgiving myself. So, Daddy told me to pray and ask God to help me to forgive myself."

He heard Altar but kept seeing the face of the one who betrayed him.

"What if someone has done wrong to you?"

Her voice changed. "I'm still working on that one."

Wolfe's eyes lifted to hers. The light showed the pensiveness in her expression. "Is this regarding your sister? The one you refuse to speak about? Or is it your former husband?"

She gave a curt nod. "Both."

The silence lingered between them, broken only by the sweet sounds of the boys as they took nourishment. Wolfe forced himself to not look away at the sight, seeing that Altar had leaned back against the headboard and closed her eyes.

She did this several times a day but within the past week, the women of the town came to visit her, each one wanting to see the babies and do what women do when they get together. When they came, he was crowded out of the house, which gave him the opportunity to explore the town and meet some of the people. Some stared at him with apprehension, mainly because of his size, but the others had been welcoming.

Mrs. Barnes continued to come, but as Altar's strength returned, she limited her visits.

Once again, he found himself thinking how strong Altar was.

His hand began to tremble again and he folded it under his arm to hide it. A muscle leapt in his jaw as he thought about the one who had taken his strength from him. How could he forgive them for what they had done?

He sat there, lost in his thoughts and memories.

"All right, His Majesty is done now."

Wolfe jerked awake, unaware he'd fallen into a light doze until he heard Altar's voice. Cautiously he moved his hand and found that the trembling had stopped. He stretched and rose, getting up to take Alpha from his wife. "I see you've eaten your fill, son. Again."

The baby gurgled happily, and he and his wife shared a tired smile.

Altar had gathered Omega closer to her as he kept feeding, refusing to be rushed.

As Wolfe rubbed and patted Alpha's back he heard her begin to sing. She always did at each feeding, sometimes hymns or spirituals. She had a lovely voice.

*Soon I will be done with the trouble of the world...*

He paused in his pacing. "I didn't know you knew that song."

"Why not?"

"You were born free, and I thought—"

Altar rocked Omega gently. "It's my father's favorite song. On their wedding anniversary, he always asks Mother to sing it for him."

"Why?"

She shrugged. "They never told me. When I asked once, Mother told me to mind my own business."

Wolfe swallowed as he continued pacing with Alpha. "Please, keep singing."

He listened to her voice as she sang, soothed by it in an inexplicable way. Even when Omega finally unlatched his mouth from her breast and both boys were burped and their nappies changed, she hummed and sang it.

"Thank you," he whispered when the boys had fallen back to sleep. "My father used to sing that song and when he died, my mother never sang it. It was good to hear those words."

"I'm glad then," she whispered. "And I'm grateful to you that you're with me."

He turned to go back to the small room, when she reached out and wrapped her arms about his waist. She barely came to the middle of his chest.

Wolfe went still, feeling her softness against him for the first time. He didn't know whether to hold her or not.

"I'm so glad I'm not alone anymore."

When she lifted her head, her eyes gleamed with unshed tears. Tentatively, he lifted his hand and cupped the side of her face, smoothing his thumb over her cheek. Her skin felt incredibly silky and warm. His heart thumped wildly in his chest.

"Good night, Altar."

She turned her head and before he knew it, she kissed the palm of his hand.

"Good night, Wolfe."

"I'm so glad you're able to do this for me, Mrs. Pennington," the wealthy woman from the Eastern district said. "Oh, my apologies. I mean, Mrs. Laingsburg."

"I understood. It's taking a moment to adjust to the change myself."

"I would imagine. I plan on leaving Last Chance by the end of January so that I will be able to stay with my daughter in Chicago for the last few months before the baby arrives. By then, she'll be confined. But she—nor I for that matter—were never good with a needle. So if you can complete the entire wardrobe for the baby by then, I'll be grateful to you."

"Of course."

"And your sons are just darling."

"Thank you." Altar stood, knowing that if she didn't, the woman would never leave. "I'll be sure to deliver them to you before then."

"Are you certain it isn't too soon to ask you to do this for me?"

Altar's lips stretched into a tight, barely genuine smile as she waved the woman's concern away. "No, not at all. I'll let you know when it is complete."

The woman left the house and Altar closed the door behind her. She was thankful for the work. Her mother had taught her nearly every handcraft imaginable over the years and she was able to sell the garments she made. It was work she enjoyed, and she liked to make beautiful things.

Day by day, she regained her strength, but she couldn't visit with people for too long before she became exhausted. The boys already took up so much of her time, but she didn't mind that at all.

She sat down on the couch in the parlor to catch her breath. Her eyes quickly glancing in the basket to make sure the boys were still sleeping. They were. Their foreheads touched while Alpha's tiny foot rested on top of Omega's legs. She gave a helpless shake of her head. Maybe Alpha really was the eldest.

As the weeks progressed, the twins' color had deepened to a warm chestnut brown. Their heads had rounded out, so they no longer had that funny, funnel-shaped point underneath the silky, riotous curls. They were both more active now, Alpha especially. Whenever she held him, his arms and legs flailed out, jerky and erratic. He made more noises than his older brother.

Omega, her precious Omega preferred to watch everything. Often, he would lie still, his grayish eyes bulged with wonder as he took in the world around him. Her sons, so tiny, so small, and already they had such personality.

She thanked God she was their mother.

How could she have ever not wanted to have a child?

She bent and kissed their foreheads before she straightened and tried to do some housework for the first time in a little over a week.

Wolfe was right. With her sons, she'd never be alone again. At least, not for a long time.

Neither was she alone whenever she was with Wolfe.

Altar paused in her cleaning. Before Elbert's death, she'd felt more alone in his presence than in his absence. The chasm between them loomed as wide as the river. They'd rarely talked anymore. Then again, they hadn't had much to say in the beginning when they first wed.

Picking up the rag once more, she went on dusting the furniture. Wolfe had gone into the town, but he would be back soon. Altar found herself with her ear turned toward the door, listening for his familiar tread.

She never listened eagerly for Elbert's footsteps. Quite the opposite. She couldn't wait for him to leave for his duties at the ranch outside of town. He'd leave long before the sun rose in the air and came home just as it began to set. It had always been a relief to see him leave.

Unlike Elbert, Wolfe was considerate of her, almost to a fault. He tried his best to maintain some sort of decorum as if they weren't married now, which she found both humorous and strangely sweet.

Elbert had considered her position as his wife as another word for his property. To do with what he pleased. When she objected to his taking on duties as an agent with the mining company, he had ignored her protests. Elbert was the head of the house and that was that.

Though her dead husband had never been unnecessarily cruel, there had been a streak of meanness in him. Especially that night when—

"He's gone now," she said out loud, cutting off the memory.

"Who's gone?"

She gasped, her hand fluttering to her heart. She turned around to see Wolfe had entered the room. "I didn't hear you come in."

"I can see that." He arched a brow. "You were just standing there."

Her face warmed. "I was thinking out loud about something. Did you mail the letter to the mining company?" Anything to distract him from what she'd said.

"I did. I hope we hear back from them soon." Taking off his hat and coat, he hung it on the coat tree. His dark eyes shone with excitement. "I talked to a woman in town. She also lost her husband in the blizzard, and she may allow me to lease the warehouse across the street."

"That's promising."

"I think so, too. If she lets me lease the warehouse, I'm going to set up the shop there for the time being. It's time I provide for us."

"When Elbert died, he left me with a small, tidy sum."

Wolfe shook his head. "I won't accept another man's charity for his wife. You can use that money as you see fit."

"I see."

Wolfe scraped his hand through his hair. His gaze roved over the room. "Where are the cubs? Are they sleeping?"

She nodded, liking the way he referred to the boys. "They're in the parlor."

"Oh good." He stretched his arms and yawned hugely. The action drew attention to his wide girth. Why was she always watching him lately? Even when Elbert courted her, she wasn't aware of his physique as she was of Wolfe's. Was it because of his size? He reminded her of her father in a way. Horace was also tall, nearly the same height as Wolfe. Whereas her father had a lean frame, her husband's body was broader. Thicker.

"I love my cubs, but they've not let us sleep for more than a couple of hours a night."

The rest of the evening went along pleasantly as they shared a dinner that Wolfe made, as she wasn't quite up to cooking for them just yet. She nursed the boys afterward, and she was pleased to see that Wolfe had finally gotten over his awkwardness about it. After which, they played with the children for a while, changed their nappies, sang, and rocked them to sleep.

They spent the rest of the evening as they had since their marriage—sitting quietly before the fire, Wolfe reading the Bible as she knitted the first of the baby wardrobe.

Later that night, Altar tossed and turned. Although she was healing, there were moments of discomfort that she experienced.

Heather had taken out the lidded chamber pot only that afternoon. Now Altar wished that she hadn't since she could use it in privacy.

Grimacing that she'd have to go outside late at night to use the outhouse, she pushed the blanket away and grabbed a thick robe. Checking on the boys in the basket, they were still asleep. She opened the door to her bedroom and went to go out the door when she stopped and sucked in a deep breath.

"Altar? Altar, is everything all right?"

She bit back a moan. "I'm fine, I just have to go to the outhouse."

She tried to walk again but stopped, closing her eyes once more as the discomfort increased.

"What's wrong?"

She opened her eyes to see his body silhouetted in the darkness. "Nothing I'm just—"

He came toward her and lifted her into his arms. "Wolfe, what are you—"

"Hush, Altar and let me help you."

She did as he said, leaning into his strength as he carried her outside to the privy. The moon was bright, and there wasn't a lot of snow to hinder their way there. Above them, the stars sparkled in the heavens. As the light snow crunched under his feet, she felt as if they were the only people in the world.

Altar shivered in the gentle, cold wind, but Wolfe radiated a heat all his own. He held her tighter and she burrowed deeper into his warmth. The beat of his heart pulsed against her cheek.

Setting her down before the door of the outhouse, he gave her a little push. "Go on, I'll be here."

Altar stared up into his moonlit face. Elbert would have never done this for her.

"Thank you."

When she finished her business, she felt much better. Wolfe was still there and without another word, he lifted her back into his arms and carried her into the house and to her bedroom, where he set her down. Checking on the boys, she saw they were still sleeping although Alpha was beginning to stir, which meant it was close to feeding time.

"Altar, next time don't be embarrassed about such things."

"I can't help it. Some things aren't meant to be shared."

"I disagree. I may not understand, but I'm here to help you however I can. When we married, I swore before God that I would take care of you."

She swallowed. "Wolfe, I—"

He trailed his finger along the side of her face. "And I will. I promise you that."

# Chapter Six

"Are you going to the New Year's Eve party?" Lisa Speciale asked several days later when she came to visit. Wolfe had gone out on business again. Altar enjoyed having Lisa come visit her.

She glanced up from her sewing, a frown on her face. "I'm not sure."

The New Year's Eve party had been discussed among the women. Some of them would be going with their new husbands that had come into town within the past few weeks. Others saw it as an opportunity to get away from the tragedy.

"If you're worried about the boys, don't be."

Altar arched her brow. "Why not?"

"I'll be more than happy to stay with them and keep them company." Lisa lifted Alpha into her arms, cooing at him and making odd faces. Omega watched from his place in the basket, content as always to observe while Alpha made a sound of glee.

"I don't know..."

"You should do it, Altar. You've been in the house for some time. Christmas is in two days and then after that, the New Year. Wouldn't it be fun for you and your husband to get dressed up and go to a party?"

It did sound like fun. When she was married to Elbert, they rarely went out, even if just to visit someone else in town. He usually wanted to stay home.

"I'll talk to Wolfe about it and let you know."

"I think I know what he's going to do." Lisa's eyes twinkled as she cradled Alpha and rocked back and forth in the chair. "He's going to hogtie you to his arm and run as fast as he can to the hotel."

Altar laughed. "You think so, eh?"

"Why wouldn't he when he'll be dancing and enjoying his time with you?" A shrewd, knowing look entered Lisa's eyes.

"What are you talking about?"

"Now, don't get upset with me, Altar, but you know me. I like telling things the way it is."

This didn't sound good.

"We all know how Pastor Collins forced you to marry because Wolfe helped you bring the boys into the world. When Wolfe married you, he saw you as a mother. I know you're not sharing a bed right now, but don't you think it's time he saw you more as a woman?"

Altar stared at Lisa, wondering how that woman knew.

As if she heard her unspoken question, Lisa shrugged. "When you're as old as me, you can read people like books. He's a good man, isn't he?"

"Yes, he is," Altar stated slowly.

"I could tell from the first time I met him. Nothing like your first husband, is he?"

"Hardly."

Ever since that day when he'd taken her out to the outhouse, Altar noticed a change in their relationship. It frightened her somewhat, but she started to feel closer to Wolfe. Every morning, they started the day together, whether caring for the boys or eating breakfast at the table. Sometimes they chatted or sat together in a companionable silence. The more she got to know Wolfe, the more she appreciated him in so many ways.

He wasn't an idle man, so he kept himself busy. The widow allowed him to lease the warehouse and he'd spend half the day there, fixing it up and setting up the shop to suit his needs. He'd gone through the inventory left behind and then went to the mercantile to order whatever other implements he needed for the blacksmith shop.

When he wasn't doing that, he spent the remainder of the day making a crib for the boys. He wanted to have it ready by the first of the year. She had suggested that they order one from the Sears catalog, but he wanted to make it himself.

"Those are my cubs," he'd told her. "I want to do this for them. Maybe teach them when they get a little older."

She loved it, simply loved it, when he referred to Omega and Alpha as his cubs. He was their father in almost every sense of the word, and she liked that he took that responsibility seriously. He loved both boys equally but somehow, Alpha was his precious. While she held Omega, he'd take Alpha and play as if they were in a world of their own. When Alpha got cranky, only Wolfe could soothe him back to calm again.

"I hope we don't turn them into Jacob and Esau," she joked one night as they played with the children.

Wolfe arched his brow. "I should hope not! I'd have to be blind and on my deathbed before that happens."

They shared a laugh and Altar's heart had fluttered at the sight of his grinning handsome face.

Lisa's words lingered long after she left. Did Wolfe only see her as a mother? Their first encounter hadn't done much to give him a different view of her. She'd been afraid, lonely, and in pain. These weeks since then must have solidified that in his mind.

Goodness knows, she didn't see Wolfe as only a father for her children, although that's what she wanted when she wrote to him. There was an awareness of her husband that never existed before, and she wasn't sure what to do with it. Once, she passed his room and saw him changing his shirt for dinner. The quick glimpse of his bare chest sent waves of heat scorching her face.

Elbert never looked as fit as that. Elbert had never made her feel breathless or uncertain. Her first husband never gave her a reason to check her appearance like she did when she knew that Wolfe would be coming back home from his work.

Did Wolfe only see her as a mother? If he did, was she content with that?

Going into her bedroom, she opened the closet and retrieved the case that held the dress she'd thought about earlier. She took it out of the wrapping paper and held it up. The burgundy skirt flowed down in a lovely cascade of fine material while from the waist up, the cream-colored shirt bore gold buttons and threading. On the wrists was an intricate design of lace the same color as the skirt. Her father had bought it for her before they went away with Temple and she'd never worn it.

"Wear it for a special occasion," he'd told her.

What would Wolfe think if he saw her in this dress? Would he like what he saw, or would he dismiss it?

She wanted him to see her as a woman. A woman that he could desire as any other man would. Even when he mentioned about their marriage being a real one, he'd only wanted her as the mother of his children. And yes, while she'd concluded that she wanted to be the mother of his children, she now realized she wanted more.

Much more.

A memory unfolded from a few years ago. She had come upon her mother and father locked in a passionate embrace in the kitchen. She heard him whisper to her mother, "You're still the sweetest butterscotch I'll have."

She'd rolled her eyes and left but the image had stayed with her.

Yes, she would go to the party and yes, she'd do what she could to make Wolfe see her as more than a mother, but also as a wife.

⁓⁓⁓

"Mr. Laingsburg, your package arrived."

Wolfe smiled at the pretty postmaster. "Mrs. Thornton, thank you. I hope you're doing well today."

The woman smiled, but it didn't reach her eyes. Though she tried to hide it, he could tell she had a cloud of sorrow wrapped around her. From what he had gleaned from Altar, Mrs. Thornton was one of the widows who lost her husband in the blizzard. She wasn't taking his death well.

"I am, thank you. How is Altar doing with the twins?"

"My wife's doing well," he replied, taking the small brown package and the small stack of letters from her hands. "The boys are just getting bigger and bigger."

"That's good to hear," Mrs. Thornton said in a dry tone. "Well, have a good day, Mr. Laingsburg."

"And you."

Leaving the postal and telegraph office, Wolfe tucked the package he'd been waiting for into his coat and headed back toward the warehouse he had rented within the last two weeks. Seeing women like Mrs. Thornton, and others who had lost husbands, he felt strange for thinking this, but he was glad there wasn't any lost love Altar had for her first husband.

The package burned the front of his body as he walked into the chilly winds. What would Altar think of it? Would she like it? He very much wanted his wife to like the gift he had gotten for her.

Wife. A Bible verse the preacher who taught him and a few of the other slave children to read came to mind. *Whoso findeth a wife findeth a good thing, and obtaineth favour of the Lord.*

When that incident happened months ago, he honestly thought his life was over. Now, in the past five weeks, his life had taken a turn he never saw coming.

Last Chance was aptly named. Wolfe believed he had received his last chance at a different life by living here. The town wasn't named for that reason, of course. It was the last stop before the stagecoach entered the mountains.

Every day, new faces showed up, mostly men who had answered a widow's letter. The mail-order grooms had come from all over. Men who had taken a chance for one reason or another to see if they could start new lives in this town.

As Altar healed, he was glad that they lived in the town. Although he'd grown up on a plantation, he never liked rural living. When he entered the urban areas, he much preferred the bustle of town life.

He was learning that physical strength wasn't everything. It could only go so far before someone came along and betrayed you. There was always someone stronger and better.

He'd learned that the hard way.

Wolfe shook his head. It wasn't time to rehash the past again. Whenever he did, it only soured his mood.

Today of all days, he didn't want that.

IIe tugged his hat over his ears, anxious to get back to the warmth of the house. When Altar told him about Elbert's position as a salt agent, he wrote a letter to the company, notifying them of his death, as well as asking for the opportunity to take over deliveries in the area. At first, he thought she would take offense to his stepping into the shoes of Elbert, but when she merely shrugged, he fully understood that Altar had no lost love for the man.

What had the man done, he wondered. Altar stated he didn't harm her physically but what would make her become so detached from him?

"You shouldn't complain, Wolfe. Not at all."

After all, Altar was his wife now. He had an opportunity to see if he could stir her to have feelings for him. And he wanted her to feel something for him. It was becoming more difficult to distance himself from her emotionally.

She made a wonderful mother, but he was seeing her as a woman. Did she know that? When she had written, she had expressly stated she wanted a father for her child. That was all well and good. No matter what he felt for Altar, which he had to admit he couldn't define, he knew he was already loving the boys and saw them as his own.

They had changed so much in these short weeks. Stronger and more alert, they took an interest in their surroundings. Omega was the quieter twin while Alpha was more likely to scream for anything. Alpha relaxed more when Wolfe was there to hold and rock him to sleep while Omega watched from the protective grasp of his mother.

It seemed as if both boys had their favorite parent, but the bond between them was real.

Wolfe never knew if he wanted to be a father, but now, he couldn't see his life without the boys in it. Yes, they woke up in the middle of the night demanding their nourishment. Sometimes they got sick on his clothes or made a mess of their nappies. There were days when they both screamed to the top of their lungs.

It didn't matter. He loved his sons and thanked the Lord Almighty above that He had chosen him to be their father.

He looked both ways before running across the street, seeing the roof of his home like a beacon in the sky. What did Altar think? Was he being a good father?

As he neared the house, he noticed a dark figure standing before it. He frowned.

He cupped his hand around his mouth and called out, "Hello!"

The figure turned but he couldn't see the face. A gust of wind blew then, shrouding his vision with snow. The hairs along his neck rose. Why was someone standing in front of his house?

Wolfe ran the rest of the way, praying silent pleas to the Lord that He would protect his family. Of course, he could have entertained other ideas for the figure to be standing there, but he didn't pretend to consider them.

Someone was watching his house.

Why?

He started to run, his feet eating up the short distance between the unknown figure and his home. "Hey!"

The person turned, lifted a hand, and then darted away.

Now he knew something was wrong. If the person had been there for a visit or to ask a question, they would have waited for him to arrive, or knocked on the door. They simply wouldn't just be standing there.

Nor would they have run away.

His heart leapt into his throat. He had to protect his family.

But how could he when his strength was gone?

The fear that had lain dormant for months began to surge like the waves of the ocean. Since his birth, he had been given a wonderful ability. His own carelessness and misplaced trust had caused it to be torn away.

His hand shook as he reached for the door and flung it open.

"Altar! Altar!"

He slammed the door shut. "Altar!"

His heart thudded slowly as if it beat through molasses. A roar sounded in the space between his ears. Where was she?

"Altar!"

She came running out from the bedroom, her face wrinkled. "Wolfe, what is it? What's happened."

She was all right!

The relief was so great that he sagged against the door, heaving as if he'd run a mile instead of a few blocks.

"Wolfe? Wolfe, what is it? What's wrong?"

He had a hard time catching his breath. "I thought—"

She reached down and took his hand, the one that shook, into her own. "Wolfe, you're trembling. What is it?"

No, he didn't want her to see him like this. Weak. Cursedly weak. He snatched his hand away, and the hurt look in her eyes sliced into the center of his chest. He didn't mean to hurt her.

"I saw someone outside the door, just staring at the house."

Altar's brow lifted. "And?"

"When I called out to them, they ran away."

Comprehension settled on her face. "I see."

"I was worried that something may have happened to you. If someone wanted to just visit, they would have come in and did so. But when I called out, they ran away. And I knew."

"Knew what?"

His breathing had eased, and he pushed himself away from the door. "I knew they weren't up to any good."

## <u>Chapter Seven</u>

The incident soured the mood for the rest of that evening. When they sat down to dinner, the camaraderie they usually shared was gone. In its place was a stony silence that sat unnatural on her husband.

What was wrong? Why was Wolfe acting like this?

In all this time, she'd never worried about his actions with her, not since that first day when he came to her aid. Had all his kindness, consideration, and everything else been an act? For what reason?

It wasn't that she didn't share his concern about what had happened. Why would someone be watching her house? They weren't wealthy or had anything of monetary value. Yes, they had some funds saved but it wasn't anything to steal over.

So why?

The children must have been aware of the change as well. They were silent in the basket, their eyes wide but with worried little frowns on their faces. More so than that, Omega's arm had somehow reached out and he held Alpha. Almost as if he were trying to protect him.

Altar pushed the food back and forth on her plate, her appetite gone. Even so, why had Wolfe suddenly pushed her away? Why did he sit at the table, moody and pensive? They should be talking about this, not sitting here as if they were strangers.

*But we are strangers,* said a voice in her head reminded her. *You've only met him almost a month ago. You were forced to marry him. How well do you know him?*

Doubts, old doubts that she had long buried, came back to the surface again. Elbert had pretended to be one way until she found out differently. Was the same thing happening with Wolfe?

She decided to break the silence and try to act as if everything was normal. "Did you hear back from the mining company?"

He gave a start and looked up at her. His eyes were dark and inscrutable. "I don't know. I did get some letters from the post office, but I forgot to check them."

"Well, do you want to do that now? I'll take care of the dishes."

Wolfe let out a huge sigh and pushed himself away from the table. "Yes, I should do that. I'd like to see if I can take over the deliveries for the town. It'll be another way to provide for the family."

The heaviness in her heart eased up somewhat when she heard that. At least whatever it was that was wrong, he was thinking of them as a family. It lifted more when she saw him pick up the basket from the table and carry it with him when he went out of the kitchen.

Maybe the incident had simply put him in a bad mood. They had nothing to worry about. Last Chance was a close-knit community. If anything were untoward, the town would come together and work it out.

Feeling somewhat better, she washed the dishes and put the leftover food into the ice box. She wiped down the table and swept the floor, tidying everything. Taking off her apron and hanging it on the nail on the wall, she walked out of the room and went into the parlor.

Wolfe stood in the center of the room, the children's basket on the small table by his side. His hand was shaking violently.

"Wolfe, what's wrong? Your hand is shaking."

He jumped and hid his hand behind his back. A snarl erupted from his mouth and he yelled, "Get out of here!"

The children screamed in fear while Altar stood there, gaping at the rage on her husband's face.

*It's happening again. Oh, dear Lord, it's happening again.*

"What's happening again?" Wolfe snapped, his chest heaving up and down.

She wasn't aware she'd spoken out loud. But now, she didn't care. "I've been fooled again by a man."

Wolfe closed his eyes. "Wait, Altar. It's... it's not what you think. I'm sorry."

"No, Wolfe. I don't want to hear your excuses. I don't want your apologies. I want you out of here."

She dashed across and grabbed the basket with the screaming babies. "I won't do it again. You're just like him."

"No," Wolfe gasped out, and the rage that had contorted his face left, slackening his features with a great weariness. "No, no, please Altar. Let me explain."

"There's nothing you can say. I've heard it all before."

He took a step toward her, but she stepped back, her grip on the basket firm and hard. "Stay away."

"Altar, I swear to you, I would never harm you. You must know that."

Some part of her did. A part of her that wasn't lost in maternal instinct and self-preservation recognized that Wolfe wasn't the type of man to behave like Elbert had.

The children still screamed, their cries beating the tense air between them. Wolfe looked down at the screaming boys and his face crumpled.

"Oh, dear God. I've made them cry."

Tears beaded in the corners of his eyes. Altar stared, shock going through her system. She had never seen a man cry. Ever. Not even her father although her mother had said that her father had cried once over her.

"Please let me explain, Altar." Hastily, he wiped the tears from his face. "Please, bring them back to me and I'll explain it to you all."

Warily she watched him, torn between what she saw and what she was remembering. Then, she took in a deep breath and came back into the parlor. Wolfe gazed down at her and then the boys.

"Please."

Altar set the basket on the table and she picked up Omega while Wolfe took Alpha into his arms. The boy screamed louder, and another tear slid down Wolfe's face. "I can't believe I did this. I didn't mean to make them fear me."

"My mother always believed that babies have a greater understanding of the world than what we can grasp or that we give them credit for."

"I can believe that. Shh, Alpha," he whispered to the screaming child. "Shh, Daddy didn't mean to upset you. Shh, my son."

Omega's cries had become whimpers, but she could tell that he was soothed by Wolfe's voice. Alpha screamed more, but Wolfe kept talking to him in that soft, gentle way. A tone that Elbert never had used. He whispered over and over how sorry he was. Omega turned his head into her chest, and she patted his back reassuringly. Maybe Omega had forgiven his father.

Alpha wasn't as easily swayed and the babe's screams reached a kind of crescendo, splitting the air like shattered glass. Still Wolfe talked gently to him, still rubbed his back and soothed. Still rocked him back and forth in the tiny parlor room, asking forgiveness.

Altar's heart softened. He wasn't Elbert. Something must have happened to make him react this way. Something not related to the incident of the stranger standing outside their door.

"I love you, my son," Wolfe kept saying, "Daddy didn't mean to frighten you."

He kissed the babe on his temple. Alpha's cries soon died away, the red of his face vanishing as well. He hiccupped, and Wolfe rubbed his back, talking gently.

Altar glanced down at Omega. He was still awake, but quiet.

Alpha's tiny mouth gaped open wide as he yawned, and his head lay back on Wolfe's broad shoulder.

"I guess you're forgiven now," Altar said in the silence that now pervaded the room. It was different than the moodiness at the dinner table.

"I guess so," Wolfe said. He looked up at her. "Can you forgive me, too?"

It was a serious question, and as she stared at him, she wondered if she could. But then, she had to remember that Wolfe wasn't Elbert. Perhaps if she told him the truth about her marriage, he would understand.

"Do you know why I can't forgive my sister?"

"No, I don't."

She took in a deep breath. "It's because she was the one who was supposed to marry Elbert, not me."

Wolfe blinked, the white of his eyes stark against the dark of his face. "Come again?"

"You heard correctly. My sister was the one who was supposed to marry Elbert."

Taking Alpha, who had fallen asleep, he cradled the boy in his arms as he sat down. "What happened?"

The past flooded before her, obliterating the present and acting out before her as if she were living in the moment again.

"Purity—"

"Purity?"

"That's her name, Purity. Now listen."

He nodded for her to go on.

"Purity and Elbert had courted for a year when he asked her to marry him. She accepted as one would expect. My parents, although not thrilled with Elbert, still accepted that he would be a part of the family. The closer the day to the wedding came, I noticed she began to act odd. When I questioned her about her behavior, she waved away my concerns. Yet, I could not get over the thought that she was afraid of marriage. I don't know why but that's what it was.

"When I asked if something was wrong with Elbert, she insisted that there was nothing wrong with him, although she finally admitted her nerves at being married. When

I told her to call it off, she said that she couldn't.

"Three weeks before the wedding, Purity ran away, leaving a note behind that she had fallen in love with someone else and that she couldn't marry Elbert."

"I see."

"My parents were terribly upset as you can expect. Elbert, at the time, seemed inconsolable. He ranted about Purity's duplicity and the shame she'd brought upon him. He came to me one night, when my parents were out with Temple, and he unburdened his soul to me. Telling me how much he cared about Purity and the like. I thought, because my sister had told me that he was a good man, that maybe I could take her place."

"Altar..."

"It was foolish of me to think that, looking back." Her face burned in remembered humiliation. "But I thought I was doing the right thing. So, I told Elbert that I would marry him in my sister's place."

"But why?"

She glanced down at Omega, who had fallen asleep. "I don't know, Wolfe. I thought I was doing the right thing. My parents tried to talk me out of it, but Elbert was just so grateful that I was doing this thing for him."

"When did things change for you? When did you recognize he wasn't what you thought he was?"

"The day after the wedding. That next morning, I woke up and there was the strangest smug look on Elbert's face. I'll never forget it. He never said anything, but over time, as we lived together, I knew. I knew why Purity had eloped with someone else."

"Is that why you're angry with her? Because she eloped?"

"That isn't the reason, Wolfe. My sister lied to me about Elbert." She couldn't keep the bitterness out of her voice. She rocked Omega in her arms as she stared across at the fire. "I asked her if there was something wrong with Elbert that was giving her pause and she lied and said no."

"I still don't see—"

"She had a responsibility to tell me the truth. If she knew that Elbert was not honorable, not what he appeared to be, she should have had the decency to say something. I married him because I thought he was a decent man. Neither of us expected love but I thought I would at least have a comfortable marriage."

Wolfe gave her sorrowful look. "I think you're blaming her for your mistake."

"Maybe I am!" she shouted. "Maybe I am but I can't help but think if she had just said something. Had just given me some idea, some notion that Elbert wasn't—"

She blew out a breath. "Can you understand?"

He gently traced the barely-there arc of Alpha's eyebrow. "I think I can, Altar. You didn't really want to marry the man, but you did. If she had given you some sort of hint, you wouldn't have."

"Am I wrong to feel this way?"

"I don't know. I just don't know. All I do know, is that if you hadn't married him, I wouldn't be here with you. And I'll be frank, there's no place I'd rather be than here with you."

Wolfe couldn't sleep. Whenever he shut his eyelids, all he could see was the pain and anguish in Altar's face as she told her story. On one hand, he felt as if Altar's pain was more bitterness than anything else because she had entered a marriage she never really wanted. She had married for obligation, not for love.

From what he had gleaned, no one had told her to marry Elbert. No one forced her into that decision.

On the other hand, he understood how betrayed she felt. Elbert had presented himself in a way that was clearly meant to mislead. Wolfe knew it was Altar's sense of familial duty that had led her to make the decision to marry her sister's 'broken-hearted' fiancé. Elbert had played on that and used it for his own advantage.

That was despicable.

Wolfe thought about the overwhelming rancor he had received from Pastor Collins. Where was that man when Altar walked down the aisle the first time?

He pushed himself off the couch in the small room and paced back and forth. When he would have unburdened his own past, Altar had cried exhaustion and he didn't fight her. They changed the boys' nappies and then laid them side by side in their basket.

He had to tell her. She had revealed all to him. Now it was his turn.

The idea of revelation made him weak. Weaker than he was already. What would she think of him if he told her? Would she look at him in the same light?

Or would she pity him?

Bile rose in the back of his throat. The last thing he wanted from his wife was her pity.

"Dear Lord, I messed up today. Help me to make it better."

Another prayer, inadequate and short, but it was a prayer, nonetheless.

Taking in a deep breath, he walked out of the room and knocked gently on Altar's door.

"Come in, Wolfe."

He opened it and saw her sitting up, a lit candle on the night table casting a becoming glow over her body. "You're already up."

"I couldn't sleep either."

Her eyes looked large and luminous, glittering like gems. He shut the door behind him and leaned against it.

"You showed great strength earlier this evening, Altar. It takes a lot of power to be vulnerable. Something I am learning the more time I spend with you."

Her brow crinkled. "What do you mean?"

For a moment, he couldn't speak, feeling as if he was stepping out into a dark pit. How could he tell her? Would she believe him?

"Wolfe, come here."

He peeled himself off the door and came to the foot of the bed. "No, come here. I want you to lie down beside me."

Wolfe coughed. "I beg your pardon?"

She scooted over from where she sat crossed legged, and then laid down. "Come."

He was momentarily distracted as the nightgown she wore rose slightly, revealing a shapely calf. "Are you sure about this?"

"Yes, I am, Wolfe. Rest assured; I am not inviting you to my bed for connubial activity. I'm not ready for that yet."

The collar of his night shirt seemed to choke him. "I didn't think that."

"Good. Now come and lie down beside me."

He did as she asked, his weight making the bed dip. They lay looking at each other in the semi-darkness. "Now, tell me what it is you want to tell me."

"Altar, do you remember the story of Samson and Delilah?"

"I do."

"When I was growing up, my mother told me that in the same way Samson's mother had given her son to the Lord, she was giving me to Him as well. She never cut my hair and over the years, I never cut it either.

"You may not believe this, but the older I got, the stronger I became. I was doing the heavy work of men by the time I was eight. My strength only increased the older I got. My mother had instilled in me the notion that I was never to cut my hair. That it was consecrated unto the Lord. So, I never did."

"What happened?"

His stomach knotted. "When I began to work for the labor company, I met a man by the name of Cain Blackwood. He was a Negro man, tall as me and almost as big. We worked well together. Soon, we became good friends. When work would cease from one site, we would go to another. Because of my strength, it was easy for me to do the work. About the time I became a steel driver, there was talk about using the machines instead of men. Those of us who worked for the company didn't want that to happen. So there was a contest. Whoever could beat the machine, the company would then cease to use the machine and continue to keep us employed."

Altar gasped. "Oh dear! You're John Henry!"

He paused. "So you know the story?"

"Who among the Negro community doesn't know the story of John Henry?"

"Well, it's not quite the way the story goes. For one thing, I didn't die when I beat the machine. For another, there were three contests not one. The first man who tried to beat the machine died. The second one gave up. I was the third one, and I beat the machine without breaking a sweat."

His mind turned inward. "I won't lie to you, Altar. I loved the attention I received from the contest. Newspapers, reporters, everyone wanted to talk to me. When I gave my name to one reporter, he didn't like it. So, he changed it to John Henry. I didn't care though. I was basking in my fame.

"I should have known better. That pride goes before a fall. For a couple of years, I was challenged by men who wanted to see if they could best the man that bested the machine. Cain was with me the entire time. I thought—"

He took in a deep breath. "I thought that he was my friend. I truly did. I had no idea that he'd become jealous of what had happened. And he plotted against me."

"Oh no."

A soft gentle touch landed on his cheek. He grabbed her hand and held it in his own. "Cain kept up the farce for a long time. I completely trusted him. Looking back, I can see how he worked hard to gain that trust. And then, he began to ask me what made me so strong. Just like Samson, I fed him lies and each time, he'd try one of them and I'd easily break from his trap."

"No Philistines?"

Wolfe gave a weak laugh. "No, no Philistines. You have to remember, unlike

Samson and Delilah, this happened over the course of a couple of years. Then, I was given the opportunity to prove that I could beat the machine again in a contest. It would be reported in the newspapers and there were going to be a lot of people. Some people, who didn't believe I had beat the machine the first time, gambled against me.

"The night before the event, Cain came to me and asked me like he had in the past, what was the source of my strength. With Samson, he was tired of her asking over and over. With Cain, I trusted him and told him the truth."

"Oh dear."

"He must have put something in my food or drink because I fell into a deep sleep. I woke up the next morning, ready for the contest and I knew something was wrong. The strength I'd always had was gone. I felt weak. That was before I saw Cain standing in the door, the most horrific grin on his face and his hand clutching the locks I had worn since childhood. My hand shook. It began to shake that day for no reason at all. It continues even now. And I didn't want you to see that."

"Do you know why it shakes?"

"No, I don't. But ever since that day, it shakes. At the oddest moments, as if my body is still...recoiling from the betrayal of my best friend. This was the hand I used to defeat the machine and maybe...I don't know."

"What did Cain do?"

"He'd gambled against me, you see. There was a lot of money involved if I had lost or if I had to decline entrance into the contest. I declined."

"I'm so sorry, Wolfe."

He kissed her palm as she had done for him that night. "Strength and being strong was my life. It was all that I was. What was I now without my strength? My hair, the symbol of that strength was gone. My reason for being? Gone. I had nothing else.

"What made it worse, Altar, was that I thought Cain was my friend. I discovered that he wasn't..."

Altar moved and before he knew it, she had wrapped her arms around him. "I'm so sorry."

"I have tried to forgive him. I really have. But I can't. He cut my hair, and took away my strength, and I don't think I can ever forgive him for it."

He felt her lips kiss his forehead, and he shuddered at the sensation.

"Then, when I thought I lost a reason for being, I answered a letter from a woman who wanted a father for her child. I met a woman who allowed me to understand what real strength is. A woman who knows that strength isn't a physical thing, but a state of mind.

"I met you."

"Wolfe."

Of their own volition, his arms came up behind her and he drew her even closer, feeling the press of her body against his own. "When I saw that person, whoever they were, outside your door, the fear that I would not be able to protect you came over me. I am afraid I am not strong enough to do what a man should do, which is to take care of his family."

"You know something? You don't have to be strong on your own. We have a God whose strength we can rely on."

A jolt went through him. "Altar."

"You read that verse a few nights ago. Remember? 'When I am weak, then He is strong.'"

The words hung between them. That and something more. Wolfe could almost feel every inch of his wife's body pressed against him. Their legs had tangled together and something very intense moved all around them.

"Wolfe, I—"

Alpha whimpered just then, and the spell that had lingered over them broke. Suppressing his disappointment, Wolfe drew himself away. "I'll get His Majesty for you."

He painfully loosened his hold from his wife and drew away to Alpha.

When he lifted the boy up into the air, he could have sworn the boy had given him a smirk, although he knew that was impossible. Even so, Wolfe played into his own fancy as he said, "I guess that's my punishment for earlier, huh?"

# Chapter Eight

Altar didn't know when the last time was that she enjoyed a Christmas like this.

Wolfe had awakened her with breakfast, and they sat in her bedroom as they had done when he first came to her rescue. She sensed the air between them had changed for the better. When he revealed his loss of strength to her, she understood him in a whole new way.

The boys had forgiven them, and they moved about energetically as the day went on. When it came time to exchange gifts, she shyly gave Wolfe a few pairs of knitted socks in different colors and a sweater.

Wolfe, trying on the sweater, gave her a nod of approval. "Now you'll have to make all my shirts, Altar. I can never find one at the stores that fits me perfectly like this one does."

She blushed. "Of course, I will."

For the boys, she'd made stuffed animals, one shaped like a bull and the other like a wolf. She gave the wolf doll to Omega and the bull to Alpha. Neither of them cared much about it, but Altar figured it was the thought that counted.

"I have something for you, too," Wolfe told her.

He handed over a gaily wrapped small box. When she opened it, she gasped. "Oh, Wolfe!"

It was a gold necklace that had the symbols for Alpha and Omega as charms.

"Oh, this is so beautiful!"

"Do you like it?" he asked anxiously.

"Please, help me put it on."

He did so, going around the back and lifting the necklace over and under her hair. His fingers softly abraded her skin.

"I love it," she said turning around. "How can I thank you for such a wonderful gift?"

A dark, intimate look appeared in his eyes. "I can think of something," he replied in a low voice.

Her heart leapt within her chest. "Really?"

"I know you don't love me, Altar," Wolfe said, making her head draw back in surprise. "I don't expect you to. But I wanted you to know that I've come to care and love you within such a short time. I don't ask that you love me back, but I do want to spend my life trying."

"Wolfe, I—"

"But if you'll let me kiss you just this once, I promise, I won't ask again until you're ready."

"How do you know that you love me, Wolfe? We've not known each other for long."

"I know because you've given me a new reason to live. Only love can do that."

Altar reached up and caressed his face. "Well, I guess I can safely say that I think I love you, too. I honestly don't know what love is, but I know what it isn't. What I felt for Elbert was nothing remotely like love. What I feel for you is different."

His head bent. "Can I have one kiss?"

She raised her arms and lifted herself on tiptoe, her eyes drifting shut as she felt Wolfe's breath flow on her face when the door suddenly slammed open.

"What the—!"

A gust of wind blew, and three men barreled through the door. They all wore bandanas on the lower half of their faces while their hats obscured all but their eyes. Wolfe shoved her behind him, his body tense as the men slammed the door.

"Where is it?" one of the men who wore a blue bandana rasped.

"Hurry, we ain't got all day," another wearing a red bandana said.

"What do you want?" Wolfe said.

"Where's the deed?"

"Deed? What are you talking about?" Altar trembled as she hid behind Wolfe's back. Thank God the boys had fallen asleep and were safely in her bedroom.

"The deed to the mine." The third man came forward, wearing a yellow bandana on his face. "We know that low life stole the deed, and we want it back."

"Stay away from my wife," Wolfe growled.

"We don't give two figs about your wife. We just want the deed."

"What deed?"

"The deed Benjamin stole from us."

Altar's mouth fell open. "I don't know what you're talking about." Who was Benjamin?

"Don't play foolish," the first man who charged in, the one in the red bandana stepped forward. "Benjamin stole that deed from the old man's hand three years ago when we robbed that stagecoach. Plucked it right out of the old man's hands right before we killed him and the rest of his family. We were supposed to sell it and split the proceeds, but that two-timing tub of guts hightailed it out of there, and we ain't seen him since."

Peering around Wolfe's shoulder she asked, "Benjamin? Who is Benjamin?"

Yellow Bandana snorted. "You married him, didn't you?"

A fine trembling overtook her. "I-I—my husband's name was Elbert."

Red Bandana made a scoffing sound. "Figures. He even used the old man's middle name. Now look here, we don't wanna hurt you, but we ain't leaving without that deed."

"I don't know what you are talking about." Her mind was still reeling from what she was learning. Wolfe kept her safely behind him, but she could tell he was as tense as a coiled wire.

Elbert? Elbert was a murderer? It seemed impossible to believe. "Wait, how did you find me?"

Blue Bandana coughed. "How do you think? We got this one's letter. Ain't nobody ever found the bodies. Far as folks is concerned, the old man and his family is just missing. But we been checkin' his letters and the like for years. When we finally got his letter, we knew exactly where to come."

Altar squeezed Wolfe's arm. A few things that hadn't made sense flooded to the forefront of her mind. Elbert had insisted on taking her name instead of having her take his own. At the time, she thought it strange. Now, she could see why. If Elbert's surname was distinctive, he could be found.

The way he was always the one to deliver the salt, making sure no one else knew the location of the mine. Whenever she had asked him, he simply told her it was in Indian territory. Wasn't that what she told everyone else?

Oh, dear God! This couldn't be happening.

"Please, just leave. I don't know anything about the deed. He never told me anything."

"I don't buy it." Yellow Bandana took a step toward them.

"Don't come any closer," Wolfe warned. "Now, my wife told you that she doesn't know what you're talking about so I suggest you turn away and leave before anyone gets hurt."

Yellow Bandana cracked a laugh. "Lookee here! He thinks he can take on three of us at the same time."

Wolfe trembled and Altar gripped his arm. She didn't want him to get hurt. "Wolfe, just—"

Red Bandana snorted. "I'm sick of this."

All the men lunged at them. Wolfe shoved her away and in a split second the men were on him. She screamed, "No!"

*Dear Lord, just one more time, give me your strength. Just once more.*

That was all the time Wolfe had to pray before the men leapt on him. In that moment, he felt vitality course through him, remembering the strength that only God had given him.

*Thank you.*

With an almost cool detachment, he began to beat the men back. One punched him in the face. He hardly felt it, but he sent an unrepentant fist into that man's jaw. Another man tried to hit him in his stomach, but he shoved him away while tackling the other one.

He moved, he punched, and kicked. He was fighting for more than he ever had before.

Not for his own glory, but to protect his family.

Wasn't that the reason for strength in the first place?

Before he knew it, all three men lay on the ground, unconscious. The bandanas had fallen away to reveal their faces.

"Oh Wolfe! Wolfe!"

Altar threw herself into his arms, her kisses raining over his face. He lifted her up and crushed her to him, drowning himself in the sensation of her sweet embrace. "I love you," she said over and over. "I do. I promise you."

He kissed her again, quick and rough and much too short and then let her loose.

"You have to go get the sheriff. I'll stay here and take care of these lowlifes."

"What about the boys?"

Wolfe gave a curt nod. "Don't worry, nothing's getting by me. Nothing."

When the sheriff came and took the men away, who had all been tied up nicely and trussed like turkeys, Altar came and held him in her arms again.

"I've never seen anything like what you did. Are you the strongest man alive?"

Wolfe lifted her into his arms and kissed her. "Only for you."

### *A week later – New Year's Eve*

Wolfe twirled Altar around, dancing to the lively music. The hotel was crammed with people, talking, laughing, and enjoying themselves. Wolfe met more of the men who had come to Last Chance as mail order grooms. The women greeted and admired each other's gowns and clothes.

It was a festive time, but Wolfe only had eyes for Altar.

He had always known she was beautiful but on this New Year's Eve, she shone like a star. Her hair was braided in an intricate pattern that Lisa had helped her with, along with getting dressed for the evening. Somehow, he had found a nice shirt and pants that fit his broad frame.

When he looked in the mirror, he noticed that his hair had grown much longer than it had before. The strength that God had given him to protect his family on Christmas Day stayed with him. Every night, before bed, he gave God thanks for restoring his ability.

He would never use it for selfish gain or notoriety ever again.

The music ended and a familiar voice called out. "Everyone, gather around and listen." Wolfe turned, along with Altar, his arm locked around her waist as she leaned into him. The room quieted.

Pastor Collins' smile encompassed the whole room as he said, "It's my pleasure to announce that we're having a wedding tonight. You know the weather can be contrary, so we better make use of the nice day we've had and conduct the wedding for Claire Braden and Ethan Freemont. If you don't mind, we'll have the wedding now and then a special dance for the bride and groom."

Wolfe and Altar shared startled glances as they saw the faces of the soon-to-be- bride and groom as they met the preacher's announcement. Amid the cheers that went on around them, Altar said in his ear, "You don't think that—"

"I do," Wolfe replied. "I do."

They joined with the others as the party became a wedding ceremony. As the preacher went on, Wolfe thought back to two days ago when the sheriff arrived at their home.

"Well, it's all true. Elbert Pennington's real name was Benjamin Scotts. He was part of a gang of thieves that robbed stagecoaches. According to our prisoners, they had robbed a stagecoach and the old man in the coach had told them of a salt mine he had the deed to. A struggle ensued and Benjamin accidentally shot the wife of the man he was struggling with. The wife's father and mother, along with the husband were killed."

Wolfe had stolen a peek at his wife, seeing her drawn face and the shock of the discovery making her skin pale.

"Are you sure it was Elbert, Sheriff?"

The man shook his head in a sympathetic manner. "If you don't believe me, believe Elbert."

He retrieved a letter he had brought with him. Altar took it and read the first line: "My sin is ever before me."

A full confession of the events as the sheriff had told them. They found the deed to the salt mine, still splattered with blood. Elbert had sold the deed and deposited the money. Due to his guilt over what happened, he never touched it. He did hire himself as an agent to the mine, but the owners never looked further than the dividends they expected and thus, never asked questions.

When the sheriff had left, Wolfe took Altar in his arms as she wept.

"Ethan, you may now kiss your bride."

Pastor Collins' voice broke through on his reverie and he watched as the groom tenderly kissed his new bride.

He glanced down at Altar and saw her own love for him shining in her eyes. Without conscious thought and in the middle of all the celebration, he gathered his wife close and kissed her with all the love he felt for her with every fiber of his being.

She tightened her arms around his neck, and he lifted her up, backing away from the crowd and finding a secluded corner in which to enjoy this moment. When they finally broke apart, he was breathing hard, wanting his wife but knowing it was too soon.

"Come on," Altar whispered as she grabbed his hand. "Let's go."

"Go where?"

"To our room for the night."

Wolfe froze in place. "What?"

She gave him a slow, seductive smile, her eyes filled with an intense feminine desire that made his legs nearly collapse from the heat. "Lisa is going to stay with the boys tonight. They'll be fine. But tonight, just tonight, I thought we should bring in the new year... as man and wife."

He gulped. "Are you sure, Altar? I can wait until you're ready."

She breathed in his ear. "I'm ready."

Grabbing his hand, she turned to lead him away from the crowd when he stopped her again. "Wait."

"What is it, Wolfe? Don't you want me?"

He gave a hard laugh. "You have no idea. But I should tell you. I've never... never..."

The words hung in the air. Invisible flames licked at his cheeks as he waited for her to comprehend what he was trying to tell her. When she did, her eyes widened.

Altar's delectable smile made Wolfe's heart thump faster as she said, "Well, Mr. Laingsburg. What better way to bring in the New Year than to learn something new?"

THE END

# Author's Note

I hope you enjoyed *A Groom for Altar*. The Blizzard Brides series is a collaborative work with several authors, so I encourage you to pick up the other books in the series by going to theblizzardbrides.com. The story about Altar's sister, Purity, will be coming out in June of 2021.

You can read about Altar's parents, Permelia and Horace, in *The Butterscotch Bride*, available on Amazon.

There are a couple of things I wanted to share about thoughts behind this book.

The first is that Omega and Alpha's vivid personalities represent my awe about babies. Netflix has a series called Babies. When I watched this a year ago, I was shocked that this documentary hadn't won an award (as far as I know). It's an outstanding series that shows in detail how intelligent babies are. That they come pre-programmed to be active members of society. Another intriguing idea presented was that babies are not passive observers but are instigators in their worlds. This led me to some exciting thoughts and conclusions that I hope to explore in other works I write.

The legend of John Henry is a fascinating one. It speaks to the tenacious spirit of the common man along with his constant struggle to fight against mechanisms of the machine. When researching the legend, I discovered that the man John Henry is obscure, but there are those who say he truly did exist, and he did beat the machine at the cost of his life.

Whether or not John Henry existed, his story is one of inspiration. I browsed online and saw many different titles and thoughts related to the man. In some books, he's a god, in others a mortal man, and still others a demi-god. Perhaps the take-away is that we are stronger than we give ourselves credit for.

Lastly, 2020 was a difficult and wonderful year for me. I enjoy the company of people and being quarantined had an awful effect on me. I remember at one point being so depressed that I fell into despair, a heavy blanket of sadness falling over me. I called my mom crying and carrying on. She fussed at me, told me to get it together, and talk to the Lord because "ain't nobody coming over there and you're gonna have to depend on Jesus".

It wasn't that I didn't know these things. But that great loneliness had overshadowed me. But I did what my mother told me to do. And the Lord heard me, and I realized that I wasn't ever alone.

I discovered that sometimes I use the company of others to mask my own thoughts or to avoid thinking about whatever it is I don't want to think about.

Before 2020, being alone was my greatest fear. I thought I couldn't handle it. I found myself enjoying my own company more and more until I realized that there's something to be said for learning to be comfortable with yourself.

I will always be an extrovert, a people person. I am invigorated by being with others. Yet, this year, I discovered my inner introvert and a greater reliance on God's sovereignty and His omnipresence.

Until next time, *Carpe diem*!

# Join Parker's Bodacious Readers
*Ordinary left a long time ago*

To stay conncctcd with me, join my reader's group for sneak peeks, ARC requests, fun times and more by joining my readers group on Facebook

# Works by Parker J. Cole

**Edgy Christian Romance Novels**
The Sins of the Flesh Series:
Many Strange Women (Book 1)
The Other Man (Book 2)
Vengeful Vows (Book 3)

**Sweet Inspirational Novels**
Michigan Sweet Romance Series:
The Cure
Time to Say Goodbye

**Contemporary Romance**
Java Cupid Series
Java Blend

7 Mafia Brides for 7 Brothers
Shattered Illusion *with Lynnette Roman*
Axel's Sunshine

**Sweet Historical Romance Novels**
Silverpines Series:
Wanted: Man of Honor
Wanted: Stonemason
Wanted: Fire Chief

Lantern in the Window Series:
Lantern of Hope
Lantern of Charity

The Proxy Bride Series
A Bride for Sterling
A Bride for Valentin
A Bride for Wen Hui
A Bride for Esau

The Pinkerton Matchmaker Series
An Agent for Arielle
An Agent for Brielle
An Agent for Camille
An Agent for Danielle
An Agent for Brutus

Hearts of South Dakota
Eva

The Blizzard Brides
The Butterscotch Bride (A Blizzard
Brides Companion Tale)
A Groom for Altar
*A Groom for Purity (June 2021)*

**Short Story Collection**
Wish Upon a Strawberry Shortcake

**Thriller Novel**
Dark Cherub

**Sci-fi Fantasy Romance Series**
Crowns and Worlds
The House of Haddaway

<u>Beyond the Veil</u>
Entangled with a Cyclops

**Anthology Works**
Birds of Passage Anthology: April and
Mr. Grim
Realms of Our Own: Godforsaken
Beatitudes and Woes: The Door to
Wishes

<u>WRITING AS PARKER PAYNE</u>
**Ascent of the Gem Bearers Series**
The Druid's Spear (Book One) with Lee
Thornton III